D1472345

The

Woman

in the

Row

Behind

Françoise Dorner

translated by
ADRIANA HUNTER

OTHER PRESS · NEW YORK

Originally published as *La fille du rang derrière*
Copyright © Editions Albin Michel S.A., 2004
Translation copyright © 2005 Adriana Hunter

Production Editor: Mira S. Park
Text design: Rachel Reiss
This book was set in 11.2 pt. Celeste Regular by Alpha
Graphics in Pittsfield, NH.

10 9 8 7 6 5 4 3 2 1

Library of Congress Cataloging-in-Publication Data

Dorner, Françoise
   [Fille du rang derrière. English]
   The woman in the row behind / by Françoise Dorner;
translated by Andriana Hunter.
      p. cm.
   ISBN 1-59051-186-7 (978-1-59051-186-2)
   I. Hunter, Adriana. II. Title.
   PQ2704.076F5513 2006
   843'.92—dc22

                              2005028828

ORIGINS: two hours of passion at a treatment spa.

BIRTH: pre-term.

STUDIES: brief.

VIRGINITY: forgotten.

WEDDING: white.

DIVORCE: under way.

WORK: yes.

SOCIAL LIFE: none.

MOTHER: behaves like my daughter.

FATHER: doesn't know me.

CHILD: turned down once. Never came back again.

FAMILY: see above.

HEALTH: can seriously damage pleasure.

DEATH: failed.

IT WAS MY MOTHER WHO INSISTED I write a book, so that there could be something of the family left behind. But, as there is no family, I stopped at that. And, anyway, I didn't have much to say—nothing, even. And it's no one's business. So I thought: a novel . . . a completely fictitious story. I read dozens of them over a period of several months; I thought they were wonderful. And not just dead authors, oh no: contemporary ones, good and alive, with photos and everything.

One day I listened to a novelist talking on the radio and I threw away all my pens and bought a computer, payable in twelve monthly installments. She said she did everything on the screen, and now I had a screen too. But I started playing games and surfing out there with everyone else, so I didn't actually write anything. I bought some new pens and I sat myself down every morning facing a gray wall with my sheet of white paper in front of me and pen in hand, ready to set off on an adventure, ready for sex, passion, death, motherhood, dual personalities, crime, glory, and downfall. After ten days I had just about managed to write two lines full of crossings out. I couldn't even read it so I threw everything away. As I dropped the bag into the special bin for recyclable paper, I wondered whether my rough attempts

I promise: next invitation, it will be yes. Before the guy even says a word. But just for lunch. As far as the rest is concerned, there comes a time when you say to yourself . . . actually, you stop saying anything to yourself at all.

ॐ

This morning I got a letter from China: my husband is happy. He went to Hong Kong as part of the new distribution service for the Parisian Press. He said that over there he would be able to live his fantasy with another woman for real, and that he was no longer angry with me. Or almost not. He said we would see about the divorce when he came back. If he came back—because he went on to say that for the first time in his life he felt he was in the right place, not there by mistake: he was putting down roots. The rest was written in Chinese characters. It didn't exactly cheer me up but when I read the first bit again I suppose it was reassuring. And, anyway, the stamps were gorgeous. I offered them to the old lady on the third floor, she collects them. She hugged me so tight it brought tears to my eyes. I didn't know a stamp could bring out so much emotion.

Sometimes I tell myself: don't always try to understand. It's true, there are times (and I haven't actually told anyone about this) when my throat gets tight, I feel as if I'm suffocating and I can't stop crying but I don't know why. At first I thought that it was pollution, but it can happen absolutely anywhere. I really ought to look into it. Perhaps I'm allergic to oxygen.

I caught the bus at midday. I don't use the Métro anymore since some asshole rammed me into the wall and stole my bag. I reported it but nothing ever came of it; they just told me I had been very lucky. At the time I didn't really understand why, and then I just told myself: don't always try to understand.

I got off at Père-Lachaise as usual. That's where my mother lives now. In a neutral apartment where there's nothing I recognize, no childhood memories. She moved house when I left, for practical reasons—she couldn't get up the three flights of stairs on her own anymore with her bottles of water and her bags bursting full of shopping. But she still had her pride and, officially, she moved because of the view, not the elevator. The view of the famous cemetery. After thirty-seven years behind the counter at the medicaid office she felt she deserved to spend her retirement looking out over the dead.

We had lunch together in her one-bedroom apartment, which was all neat and tidy, all immaculately polished, all lavender bleach and pine fresh.

"When the day comes when I can no longer do my housework . . ."

There is always a long silence after these words. She wobbles her head from left to right, her pretty face like an aging little girl who hasn't been ruined by this life. When I don't say anything, she goes on with her sentence:

". . . you'll be able to say it's the end. I'll never go into a home. But I don't want to be cremated, I'm too frightened of fire. Or buried. All those stories about people waking up in their coffins . . ."

And it's always the same for me: I suddenly lose my appetite, my stomach feels heavy, and I start clenching my fists.

"Can't we talk about something a bit more cheerful when we're together?"

"But you're my daughter. Who do you expect me to talk to about this? You won't abandon me, will you? You're all I have."

What about me, who do I have? Being her daughter now means reversing the roles, taking responsibility for her, defending her, sacrificing my life for her. All the things she has never done . . . or only very badly. But she has no memories of that.

That was the day she opened her little linen cupboard: The sheets and towels and all the linen neatly lined up, arranged by color. I thought of my own airing cupboard. I could fold the sheets and things away fifteen times but the whole lot would fall onto the floor every time I opened the door, just to spite me. I can hear my linen laughing. My mother took out a big cardboard box and I was instantly suspicious. I should have left straight away. She looked up with great dignity and said:

"You may not have any family, but you do have photographs. I was keeping them for you, for when I'm no longer here . . . and then I thought they might do you some good, right now. I'll go and make the coffee. I know them all by heart. When you live on your own. . . . Well, you know what that's like at the moment."

That was the one sentence too many, the sentence that kills. I should have put that cardboard box back where it came from and shut the linen cupboard. But when you're hovering between two lives, you hesitate. I was very afraid of coming face to face with the little girl I had once been. How would she judge me, now that she had grown up? I was bound to disappoint her. When she saw me she would think: is that what I turned into?

I stared at the first photo: in the park in winter, seven or eight years old. The only difference between us is that I've had the courage to cut off my braids. As for everything else, unfortunately—apart from size—I haven't changed very much. I still have the grazed knees and a Band-Aid somewhere on me.

The other pictures were of my mother: my mother and her baby from every angle. In that box my life stopped when I was eight. The teenager and the grown woman had no right to asylum in it.

I closed up the family box and looked at my father on the sideboard, in his brass frame. His expression was distant, kindly, stubborn—it depended on which angle you were looking at him from, and the time of day. One of my first memories (and one I have never tried to erase as I have grown up) is of my mother smiling lovingly, so proud of me, and leaning against the glass of the frame, whispering to him: "She's exactly like you."

I WAS NEVER THERE WHEN IT mattered. Or perhaps some-times, but no one ever noticed. Transparent, an invisible little woman—but there is an upside to that: you can watch and listen, keep it all to yourself, and gradually you forget the sound of your own voice.

I didn't miss out on everything.

A man even married me. First at city hall, then in church. All in white, even if he wasn't the first, and even if he wasn't the last. I said yes all the way through. I was so happy to be asked anything, to be recognized by a man at last, for him to give me his name . . . no longer having the same name as my mother.

The wedding night activities lasted ten minutes. I've known better, but apparently—with all the family tensions, the drink, and the friends—it can take less than a minute on the wedding night. That happened to Gisèle, so I was actually very lucky.

"Did you like that, now?" he asked me, and he meant now that we're married. I just said yes. And he went to sleep.

I didn't so much as close my eyes. I wanted to make the most of that first night not having to sleep under my mother's name. I snuggled against him and thought about my hair, which had been so perfectly lacquered for the cere-mony. I really think I used the whole bottle of hairspray. I wouldn't have liked anyone saying I was a neglected bride, but no one complimented me on my pretty, rock-solid chi-gnon. Apart from Gisèle. Mind you, she did criticize me for my choice of groom. "Frankly, you deserve better," she said. "What do you think it looks like throwing yourself at the first comer?" I didn't answer. I thought he was kind, straightfor-ward, honest, he didn't make beautiful speeches—that made a change from his predecessor, a certified public accountant who said he was getting a divorce. Well, he said that for the time it took to bed me and then over the next few weeks he proved to me, with the help of his calculator, that when you added it all up he couldn't afford to take on the alimony. My husband, on the other hand, was a man who always told the truth. He talked about it as if it were a matter of life and death. His parents had torn each other apart, betrayed each other, and lied to each other all through his childhood, call-ing him to witness: that had inoculated him forever. At first I thought it was fantastic, a man who was always true, frank, authentic—even though it did mean he didn't say very much. In fact he didn't have anything to say, but I didn't realize that until much later. You can go on interpreting silence as shyness for a long time, and imagining whole sentences when you just look someone in the eye. You think you can understand each other with snatches of words. That you don't need to talk because you're comfortable together.

For our honeymoon he took me to the Place de la Concorde and we went on the big wheel. Twice.

"Did you like that?"

"Yes."

And it was true that time. I had a feeling of freedom unlike anything I had felt before being married. Because he was there and I didn't have to say "No, that place isn't taken" to anyone, or pretend I was waiting for someone so that people would leave me alone, or lower my eyes—ashamed— when no one asked me anything. And every time our seats skimmed the ground, I flew off all over again, and no one could catch me. And with the swaying of the little pod I even felt like making love, just like that, only for a moment. I took his hand and closed my eyes, reaching my mouth toward him, but he didn't react, so I opened my eyes. My husband was terribly pale, about to throw up, so we got off and there was no third time. That was when I thought I might have made a mistake.

Then everything fell into place, and I started my life as a married woman: working, doing the housework, the shopping, the cooking, closing the shutters, and falling asleep dreaming. Dreaming of the man I had known before the wedding: anxious, sensitive, eager, shy, the man who had changed so quickly now that, as he would put it, he had "buried his bachelor days." I could have done with their being resuscitated, with him turning back into the impatient lover who would crush my fingers with his hand and keep saying the same thing every time we met: "I want to share my life with you." But I understood rather too late that, to him, sharing his life was sharing his work time.

⚮

We had to get up very early in the morning—at five o'clock. My husband would take the van to return the unsold copies and pick up the dailies from the Press Depot near Rungis. It meant he avoided the delivery charges, which saved us at least 150 euros a week. They were heavy, six or seven hundred kilos, but at least it meant half a percent less to give to the Depot. Then he would go and set up the kiosk before the customers arrived. He could have waited until opening time, but he made it a point of honor. Meanwhile, as usual, I would make the bed, put the washing machine on, and run over the carpets with the vacuum cleaner—a present from my mother.

One morning, as I crouched to get it out of the closet, I suddenly felt humiliated to be kneeling before a vacuum cleaner. It was February 28th. I gave it a defiant look: I won't do it today, you can stay where you are. And if my husband comments this evening, I will tell him, perhaps even with a note of insolence:

"No, I haven't done the vacuuming."

"Why not?"

"I don't know."

But I knew very well why not: all of a sudden, I no longer wanted to be like my mother, polishing, rubbing, waxing so that everything was spotless and clean. Not one crumb of life, not one crumb of bread. Place mats, bath mat . . . doormat.

As he left he said, "Don't forget to peel the vegetables." I hadn't forgotten—I just wasn't doing them. I watched the snow falling against the kitchen window. I identified with it, I felt as soft and intangible as those little white flakes. But I didn't want to come to a pathetic end like them, in the black slush on the tarmac, crushed under shoes or tires, on that last day of February.

When I arrived at the kiosk he said, "You took your time," and then he went off for a cup of coffee, and I felt very alone.

Cramped in my three sweaters and my thick down jacket, with my woolen hat pulled down to my eyes and with my fake fur boots on my feet, no one would have guessed that I was a little snowflake that sometimes landed delicately on the lapel of a coat or a stranger's cheek. It was a long time since it had snowed in Paris. For me, it was the first and last time that it snowed while I was a married woman.

ᲑᲛᲗᲦᲝ

He didn't say anything about the vegetables: he felt like pasta. He didn't notice about the vacuum cleaner. So we didn't talk. He fell asleep in front of the TV. I cleared the table. It stopped snowing.

EVEN IN SUMMER YOU HAVE to wear warm clothes in the kiosk, because we're on the wrong side of the street. The odd-numbered side, the northern side, the shady side. Still, trussed up like that, people don't really notice me, and I can watch them at my leisure. There is the passing trade, women who buy *Le Monde* and slip the special edition magazine in with it, the one entitled "Cosmetic Surgery: Where and When?" I stow them discreetly into a plastic bag; I like the silent complicity between us. Then there are the regulars: "You're so lucky, you know: at least you get some fresh air while you're at work." "Taking three days at the weekend's not enough, I'll be even more tired at the end of it! It's like an aborted holiday! But I can't do anything else, with the thirty-five-hour week. I'll have to take that extra day, I'm owed it!" "Will you be open tomorrow? Of course, you're open every day, silly me: how would people get their papers? Oh, right, not Sundays?"

Sometimes these women also talk about more personal things: headaches, children leaving home, parents reverting to childhood, husbands getting uptight, security problems in Paris, failed haircuts, blocked arteries, falling bone density, even if they turn themselves inside out trying to stay young. I don't hear all of it, but I understand them. No one listens to them at home, and you can say such intimate things to someone you will never know—that must be the same for everyone. But I really am interested, I get inside their lives and I like it. Some of them even say, What would I do without you? And they leave just as I'm about to reply.

And then there are the men.

Those who pretend to be polite—"No, please, you go first; I have plenty of time"—and who leaf through *Libération* when they're actually turning the pages of *Playboy*. I was watching them undressing the girls with their eyes one day when I realized my nipples were erect, in spite of my wool shirt and my thick cable-knit sweater. It wasn't any particular man who aroused me. No, it was the way they behaved like children who weren't allowed to do something. I would watch them secretly, almost with my back turned. At first I just found it fun, then it became a real, serious game. I knew their schedules, what time they would arrive. Sometimes I would hide their favorite magazine, and they would search for it feverishly and wouldn't dare ask me where it was. Then, I would get one out very discreetly and put it right in front of me. I would crouch down behind the counter for a minute and, when I stood back up again, the magazine would have moved slightly. They would hand me the money for their daily paper and I would give them the change, just brushing the tips of their fingers, on purpose because it gave me a little shiver of pleasure.

One day I stayed crouching behind the counter: I wanted to know what it was they were so interested in. I leafed through one of their magazines, and I found myself turning the pages more and more slowly. Beautiful women with lots of makeup, with breasts like the old nanny who used to look after me when my mother went out dancing. Just a bit higher up, that was all. Plenty of highlights, but hardly any pubic hair. Toward the end there were pictures of Oriental girls with long black hair, wearing tightly belted black coats, perched on high-heeled black shoes, with long white teeth biting into a black whip. A man asked for a copy of *Exchange and Mart*. I closed the magazine, wondering what I would look like in that outfit.

Looking back, I can see now that that is where it all started. A mundane moment of reflection that would turn my own life and my husband's fate upside down. We always think it is events that change us, but events are nothing without the little sentence that draws them out, holds them there and transforms them. *What would I look like in that outfit?* The little sentence that would topple everything over the edge.

AT HOME NOTHING HAD CHANGED: my husband would wake at three minutes to five, and by five o'clock we had made love. He would get up in a good mood then. I was happy for him but so disappointed: it had been four days and he still hadn't noticed the heart shape I had created with my pubic hair, plucking around it like the girls in the magazines.

And then suddenly, one Tuesday, quarter of an hour after he had left, I had a moment of revelation: it wasn't indifference, it was the darkness. Given that we always made love in the dark, it was perfectly normal that he hadn't noticed anything. I set off straight away, running after him to show him my surprise, he absolutely had to see it, there, right away, but I was knocked over by a car. I fell head first onto the cobblestones. The guy stopped—apparently that's pretty rare, especially at a pedestrian crossing. We were alone, just the two of us in that deserted street. I kept my eyes closed. I had never lain like that before, right in the middle of Paris, with my skirt hitched up. He leaned over me and rolled me onto my back, saying, "Mademoiselle!" in an anxious voice. I cut my breathing dead. I was frightened and, at the same time, excited: I was wearing a pair of violet lace knickers that I had spotted in *Marie-Claire*, and they weren't really intended for road traffic accidents. I heard him take a deep breath, and then he pressed his mouth over mine. A warm mouth that smelled of coffee and orange marmalade. I kept my eyes closed a long time; it didn't matter what he looked like. I thought of those women belted into all that black, and I bit his breakfast-flavored lip. He sat back up, saying:

"You bitch! Are you crazy?"

I opened my eyes and, now that I could see, everything became real again. I stood up, pulled down my skirt and walked away without apologizing. I didn't thank him, not for the coffee, not for any of it.

All I wanted to do was lie down on the ground and see if I felt that same excitement again, but I caught sight of myself in the window of a bakery: I had a huge bruise under my right eye, so I thought I should put off my second fall till later.

When I reached the kiosk I told my husband I had . . . fallen. And I said it in such a strange voice, laden with hidden meaning. But he just muttered:

"Be a bit more careful in the future. You're so clumsy . . ."

And that was that.

I was going to tell him about my surprise, but he went off to have a beer. I just felt stupid then, with my heart between my thighs.

A few days later my bruise was completely yellow with a few raised areas in red. Like a Kandinsky—it wasn't me who thought of that but a new customer. He looked at me with a smile, and said, "That looks like a Kandinsky," and

he gave me 50 euros. For his paper. It was the first time a
stranger had smiled at me as he gave me 50 euros. I got his
change wrong three times. That evening I looked through
the encyclopedia to see what my bruise looked like.
Kandinsky was a Russian painter who was granted German
citizenship, then French. He invented abstract art. After looking at one of his paintings I snipped bits of my nightdress,
mussed up my hair and went into the bedroom, as proud as
the Statue of Liberty, to slip between the sheets beside my
husband, who just nodded at my eye and said:

"I hope people don't think I did that to you!"

"You wish!" I muttered, turning the other way.

It's odd: it wasn't my voice, that husky, playful, provoca-
tive note. It came from the nightdress, from the bruise . . .
or was it from the look in that man's eye, the man who
thought I looked like a painting?

ᏀᎳᎳᎧ

. My husband went away for a week to help his brother move
house. He had just split up with my friend Gisèle, and had
decided to live in the country. So, good little soldier that I
was, I ran the kiosk all on my own. It meant I was working
fifteen hours a day, but it didn't matter: I was so tired that
the time passed more quickly. The man with the 50 euros-
smile came back every day to get his paper with his big
banknote. It was usually in the evening, at nightfall. He
would ask me for news of my bruise, and watched it gradually fade. He even wanted to touch it once. I gave him a little

slap on the hand and laughed. But on that particular day he smiled at me in such a way that I agreed to go and have a drink with him, despite being so tired. Or because I was so tired. In the end all I wanted was a tomato juice. Just for the Tabasco—I love Tabasco, it's delicious and spicy but my husband's against it, so it was a good opportunity. He ordered a Bloody Mary for me, and the sound of his voice made me disappear to the restroom so that I could say it to myself all on my own in front of the mirror:

"Bloody Mary, Bloody Mary, Bloody Mary . . ."

I found those four syllables incredibly exciting. Like when I used to say "Our Father who art in heaven" when I was fifteen, at boarding school. It's strange that there are feelings buzzing around beneath words, completely unrelated to what they mean.

When I came back, my Bloody Mary was there, right next to his, with lots of black and green olives in a bowl on the table, and even some peanuts in a silvery dish, next to a candle that had just been lit. I had never seen such a chic bar. They didn't talk about this sort of place in my magazines. The sign was so small they must have failed to notice it. He offered me a cigarette, I told him I didn't smoke.

"Just one. To taste it. My name is Jean."

And for the first time in my life I inhaled the smoke of a long white cigarette with a golden filter, and I liked it. Then he handed me my Bloody Mary.

"Here's to you."

I didn't really know what to say to that—"And here's to you," "Chin chin," "Cheers"?—and I felt a bit cluttered with my cigarette in one hand and my glass in the other. So I took another drag, took a sip of my drink with a mysterious glint in my eye, and coughed because it was strong. My cigarette fell down my blouse. I opened my mouth wide but I didn't dare scream in that bar with its soft lighting. Without a word, he slipped his hand gently inside my bra to remove the cigarette, which had burned the white lace with its little red tip. I said there was no harm done then, to change the subject, I asked how the cocktail got its name. He told me that opinion was divided: it was either Mary Tudor, the English queen, or the wife of a Soviet ambassador to London, because of the vodka. My head was reeling so I ate nearly all the olives, pits and all—I wasn't going to spit them out and, in front of him, I couldn't put my fingers in my mouth. That's what must have made him think I was hungry. He asked me if I liked wild salmon fillet.

"Oh yes," I said.

"And pirojkis?"

"Them too."

"And caviar?"

"I love it."

"I'm afraid they don't have any here."

He ordered some food. I felt jittery, excited by all those things I had never tasted. He was telling me about Saint Petersburg, talking about the scenery, the museums, the sun setting over the ice, the caviar in silver ladles, and in my head I could hear the words: *Bloody Mary who art in heaven.* One of the candles started to drip wax and I went to stand it upright, but, because I never drink any alcohol, I tipped over the peanuts. Luckily our table was a little way from the others, in an alcove. Otherwise, I might not have got down on all fours under the table to pick them up. He leaned over to help me, took my hand, and, with a completely natural gesture, put it between his thighs, over the buttons of his fly. I was a little surprised: my husband only wore trousers with zippers. The waitress brought our order and he hid my face under his napkin. By the time she left, Monsieur Jean was unbuttoned and, for the first time in my life, I found myself kneeling in front of a man who trusted my mouth and my steely little teeth.

Afterward, I got back up to eat.

Hallowed be thy name, thy kingdom come . . .

Do all men like that, except for my husband? As soon as he came home I wanted to try it on him, but he lifted my head back up and told me, almost reproachfully, that we were married. What did he mean? That from any other woman he would have liked it? I could have done with asking Monsieur Jean what he thought but since the evening with the Bloody Mary I hadn't seen him again. He must have been buying his paper somewhere else. Perhaps I had disappointed him. Or he was doing the rounds of the three hundred and twenty outlets in Paris. Women in newspaper kiosks were his fantasy.

"What's got into you?" my husband went on, his voice serious. "Aren't you happy just as we are?"

"Yes . . . of course I am," I whispered.

But I was lying. I would have liked to tell him my story with the peanuts, to let him know that I knew things now— like those women in the magazines—and that I certainly liked it. But I didn't dare, I was afraid of how he might react, afraid he would reject me. I'm always afraid of being abandoned when I disagree with someone; that's one of the reasons I never contradict my mother—or anyone else, for that matter. So, as compensation, I decided to stop using hairspray.

I started my underground life and it gradually took over. I washed my hair carefully with chamomile and it got more and more blond, and I tied it up loosely like the L'Oreal girl in one of my magazines. I told myself I was someone else. I bought myself some pink blush and I put it everywhere, and men started telling me I looked fresh as a rose. I'd always thought I was pretty insignificant so that did me a lot of good. I grew bolder: I plastered my long eyelashes with mascara like Queen Nefertiti in the new history magazine. My husband didn't notice anything, so I carried on by spreading turquoise eyeshadow on my eyelids like a female minister featured in *Madame Figaro*. With the turquoise I noticed that men stayed longer to buy their papers. They talked to me about the rain and also about fine weather, but mostly about the long lonely weekends in Paris while their thirty-five-hour-week wives were off taking the air by the sea or in the country. I would listen to them, and none of them ever guessed that they could have just kissed me on the mouth, for a good long time and really hard, without taking any sort of air apart from the pleasure of it. Well, it's their loss.

One day the lease came up on the kiosk a little further along, on the other side of the street, the sunny side. The man was retiring and luckily he was what's known as second category, like us, so that we could come to an arrangement with the next nearest outlet to take holidays. My husband didn't want to be in the first category, because we wouldn't have been allowed to close. But the sunny side of the street changed everything: a five percent rise in sales figures. We didn't think twice before crossing to the other side. My husband looked at me and said rather oddly:

"You'll be able to get a tan now too."

And it made me feel strange because the dark, shadowy side of me was gaining ground every day so a tan would be a form of camouflage.

At first our customers would turn up looking for us and we would wave to them from the sidewalk opposite, like different members of a large close-knit family who hadn't seen each other for months. Well, I'm imagining that because I only have my mother. Monsieur Jean came back one evening, but I was with my husband: no, he wasn't buying his paper anywhere else, he had just gone to plead a case out of town. After complimenting us on our change of sidewalk, he turned to my husband and, as if asking a huge favor, asked whether we could bring *Le Monde* to his office on Monday afternoons as soon as it came out so that he could look through their legal supplement. I looked at him and felt hot all over so I closed my eyes and, almost in spite of myself, I bit down on my tongue while my husband agreed: "My wife would be happy to bring it. It's a pleasure being of service." Once Monsieur Jean left he told me he had agreed to it because he admired him: Monsieur Jean always spoke to him as an equal, and was therefore a good man. He would have liked to have him as a friend (as if he had any). It felt strange that they knew each other. It wasn't remorse; it was disappointment. I would have liked to keep Monsieur Jean all to myself. But I did take some comfort from the fact that, when he bought the paper from my husband, he gave him the exact change.

⟨ᴍᴍᴏ⟩

At about seven o'clock I hurried off to the supermarket: Gisèle was coming for supper. It irritated my husband but I owed her that at least, even if bringing her into my marital home wasn't necessarily the best way to cheer her up over her divorce.

I trundled the shopping cart through every department. Seeing Monsieur Jean again had reminded me of the wild salmon fillets, but I didn't want to jumble up my emotions. What I was looking for now was some caviar. I wanted to know what it tasted like, to be on a par with him. I asked one of the salesgirls where I could find some. She told me there wasn't any point spending that much and that they didn't sell it anyway. Seeing how disappointed I looked, she took me to one side:

"Lump fish roe is just the same, except it doesn't say 'caviar' on the jar. It's like when they put *grand cru classé* on red wine—you pay for the label but it's still only red wine. You could just throw the jar away, no one will notice a thing. It's the same little black eggs, but ten times cheaper."

"What about real caviar, have you ever tried it?"

"Never. I'm not stupid."

So I took two jars of lump fish roe, and I slipped them into my cart with a knowing little nod, so that I could be clever too.

That evening I produced blinis topped with the black eggs. My husband asked what they were.

"That's caviar," I said simply, shaking my shiny blond hair.

He almost choked! I had to go and get the jar out of the garbage to show him it really wasn't expensive, and to ask him if he could taste the difference.

"What difference? I've never eaten caviar."

"Oh I have, I've been offered it a few times," I said for the pleasure of making him jealous. "But it's not worth it."

Gisèle burst into tears. She really had been depressed since her husband had left her. She couldn't bear the sight of all those little eggs. She imagined the worst: someone slicing into the belly of a mother fish, a living mother, and taking her babies. She leaped to her feet and hurled her blini out of the window with peculiar violence. I held my breath. My husband's only comment was:

"That was all we needed."

I ran to the window. No one had been hurt, the blini was draped on a windshield.

I didn't dare bring in the calf's head I had prepared. I quickly took a frozen dinner from the freezer, and gave them the rest of the blinis with a little pâté while they waited for it to heat through in the microwave.

"What sort of pâté is this?" Gisèle asked.

I was going to say rabbit, but I stopped myself just in time.

"It's organic. There's nothing in it."

"Oh! I'm glad."

She wolfed down three blinis with pâté, still making anxious hiccupping noises from time to time. But it wasn't because of my cooking. Her husband had left her to go and live in the country because she was allergic to pollen. And I felt slightly guilty: if I hadn't married, she would have stayed single. She had been so afraid we would lose touch that she married my brother-in-law. And now he was the one who got to keep their dog.

At the end of the meal I tried to break the silence by saying:

"Have you had any news?"

"None at all," Gisèle replied with an aggressive edge in her voice. Then she turned to my husband and asked, "Have you?"

He poured out the last of the wine and mumbled, "The same. But it doesn't surprise me."

That was when Gisèle snapped and, as usual, I got the worst of it.

"You made me make the biggest mistake of my life! And what was it all for? What? I'm really sorry to say this in front of you, Roger, but he never made love to me properly. Don't look at me like that, you hypocrite! I can see you don't have that sort of problem. But of the two of us—I don't want to stir up the past, Roger—but the more sexual one of the two of us . . ."

"It was rabbit pâté," I said very softly.

She fled to the bathroom and we had ten minutes' peace.

"Do you think she's sexy?"

I looked at him in amazement. It was the first time I had heard him use that word. I said I didn't notice that sort of thing and he said, "I always thought there was another woman in my brother's life. On the other hand, he would have told me. We always tell each other everything."

He cut himself a slice of bread, staring at me all the time.

"And me, what do you think about me?" I asked.

He took a good long look at me, still earnestly chewing his cheese, and I immediately regretted asking. There was only one thing I wanted: for him not to reply. But he did reply, very slowly:

"Perfect."

I felt like screaming, "I sucked off a man because some peanuts fell under the table, do you still think I'm perfect?" But I didn't say anything. I gave a stupid, modest smile, and cleared the table. Gisèle came and sat back down, holding a damp flannel to her forehead. She apologized. The anti-depressants made her aggressive, it said so on the leaflet.

"I have to stop reading those leaflets," she added grudgingly, "I get all the side effects."

"About the pâté . . . it was a joke," I said gently.

"Don't tell me I was sick for nothing."

I put the ice cream on the table and she burst into tears at the sight of her favorite dessert: vanilla and pistachio. And I was almost relieved that she was crying instead of me: the word "perfect" just wouldn't go down, it was building up a great lump in my throat. What did "perfect" mean? Nonexistent. That was what he had liked about me, and what he would soon be resenting me for, because he would get so bored.

He turned on the TV and fell asleep almost straight away. It happened more and more often, but I couldn't say anything. I was the one who gave him the new TV, last year. The one they called "home cinema." The name alone was magical, you no longer had to go and stand in line somewhere to be entertained; life-size dreams could now invade your own home. It was my anniversary present to him. Setting Hollywood up for him at home had cost me my savings toward our own house. I didn't have a clue what I was going to do this year. Why give someone a present when there was nothing to celebrate anymore?

The dishwasher wasn't working. Before we did the washing-up I spent ten minutes looking for rubber gloves to protect Gisèle's nail varnish. But I didn't find any, so she sat on a stool and we chatted while I washed the dishes. We talked about her life, about her dog who had gone off without a backward glance, her work, which she found distressing—she saw so many gum boils, rotten teeth, cases of gingivitis, and exhausted, bloated, deformed people that she felt she was turning into a monster. Then she started talking about her nails which were so long that she couldn't even make her bed anymore but she didn't want to cut them in case she met a man. I looked a little confused so she explained that she would scratch his back until he bled, and even better:

he would pay for all the others, for all those who hadn't chosen her before.

That was when I broke a glass, and I cut myself as I picked it up. I smiled furtively at the sight of my blood. I could picture a stranger's back under Gisèle's vengeful nails.

What exactly would I have done with a stranger's back?

I ran cold water over my finger for a long time but the bleeding didn't stop. Still perched on her stool, Gisèle heaved a sigh.

"You really have a problem with clotting! One day you'll bleed dry like a chicken! Have you had any blood tests? You would tell me, wouldn't you, if you had something serious?"

"Of course."

I would have loved it if, like in the old days, I had been able to tell her all my little secrets, but since her husband had left her she had a way of talking that didn't lend itself to confidences. I suddenly felt choked by all the things I couldn't tell her: the women with long black hair in the men's magazines, the Kandinsky painting, the peanuts under the table . . . I would only have made her jealous. I walked out of the kitchen saying I was going to find some disinfectant for my finger. Disappointed with myself for leaving her, I waited behind the door for five minutes listening to what she was doing. But there wasn't a single sound, so I went back in. She was still there, perched on my stool, staring at what was left of the glass. Poor thing, a caged lioness who has lost her tamer. That was why she had been my friend ever since boarding school—whatever she did, there was always something about her that made me want to take her in my arms. An apologetic loneliness, hiding beneath her aggression. I picked up the bits of broken glass.

"There's still a bit over there," she said getting off the stool.

I looked at her legs.

"Do you wear stockings now?"

"Well, I'm hardly going to get myself a man with socks!"

I saw her to the door and, before she left, she hugged me and whispered:

"You've gotten much prettier."

Again I wanted to tell her everything but she added; "It really shows that you're not lonely."

She looked at my husband who was still sleeping in front of the TV and then, as if forgiving him for something, she murmured, "Go on, wake him up. His brother would never have gone to sleep with me anywhere near him. And he didn't leave me for another woman, he just went off with the dog. If only you knew how life suddenly becomes . . ." She finished her sentence with a sigh, letting her arms drop by her sides.

"I know."

"No, you can't know! Wait till it happens to you." And she patted my cheek before stepping out into the hallway.

I went over to the armchair. Slowly, I scratched my husband's back very gently. It woke him with a start. He dropped the remote control and jumped up:

"What's got into you?"

"Nothing . . ."

"Did you want to tell me something?"

"No, I just wanted to touch you, that's all."

He unbuttoned his shirt and went to look at his back in the mirror.

"I'm going to bed. You can switch the lights off."

I watched him leave and I tidied the kitchen. Was married life always going to be like this, then? No longer seeing the other person because they're always there. No more sense of conquest, no more attentiveness, no more danger, no more lies, no more promises. . . . Moving into a house as a couple was my life's dream, it had been since I was a little girl. Obviously I had no points of reference. There had never been a man in the house—or only temporary ones, but lovers aren't the same; they're polite and they smile, because they don't know where anything is. And you have to be nice to the kid. A pat on the head, a question about school, a compliment on her braids. I was the one who opened the door, and I was the one who closed it. Hardly surprising, because I slept in the hallway. The dining room could have been my bedroom, but, as far as my mother was concerned, a dining room was sacred. Even if she did only use it on Sundays. Right up till I went to boarding school I slept on a bed that was disguised as a settee during the day, with my doll, my teddy bear, and my school bag hidden in the closet with the vacuum cleaner, all because of the women my mother played cards with in the afternoon. She wanted them to think she had another room: the "kid's bedroom" at the end of the corridor—a closed door that only housed the gas meter. And

I lived in a waiting room. I don't mean that my mother had a lot of visitors—apart from the rummy players and the one-night dancers I opened the door to—but that I was always waiting. And I still am. Except that, after my husband, I didn't think there would be anything else. Maybe it's my fault. I'm not experienced enough, I don't say what I think, or what I want to say. There's always the fear that I won't be loved anymore, if I step beyond my boundaries. Even now, I'm still just a little girl who used to open the door. But who to?

Amazed my heart isn't beating any faster, I ring the bell next to a plaque which says "Lawyer's Office." I'm shown into the waiting room, where a man and a woman are already waiting. I sit down on a large sofa and move to get up when someone opens a double door, but it isn't Monsieur Jean. The secretary glances at the three of us, then nods discreetly at the woman, who stands up and follows her. The double doors are closed. After six minutes the man leans towards me:

"Could I borrow your newspaper?"

He smells good, his hair is immaculate, beautiful suit, dreary tie. I hand him *Le Monde* and he sits down next to me. He opens the paper wide, he has beautiful hands. He says rather seriously that the law on water won't change anything. I picture his back under his finely striped shirt; I think of Gisèle, of her nails, and I laugh to myself. He turns toward me.

"Are you laughing at me?"

"No, it's my sister-in-law. She keeps her nails very long just in case she meets a man."

"She's right, you can't be too careful," he tells me, and then adds with apparent concern, "But yours are very short."

"Yes," I replied in a childish little voice that I hate.

But that's me all over: someone only has to impress me for me to become a complete dope, or should I say "perfect," as my husband calls it. So I asked him:

"Have you ever been scratched?"

"Beaten, yes. Attacked, messed up, destroyed . . . but I don't think scratched."

Not daring to ask him too many personal questions, I tried something that would give us a more equal footing:

"Is this the first time you've been here?"

"Sadly not. I'm very exposed and I don't let anything go. Every time there's a smear I take the culprit to court."

Although I felt doubtful, I told him he was right to. After a moment, I asked him what line of business he was in.

He crossed his arms and roared with laughter.

"What line of business. . . . Don't you recognize my face at all?"

"I don't know. I see so many . . ."

He raised an eyebrow, so I explained: "In the papers. I'm sorry."

"Not at all, mademoiselle."

I didn't put him right on that. I had taken off my wedding ring out of respect for my husband. Or for Monsieur Jean, I'm not sure. This man's voice did something to me, I was forgetting why I was there, or at least I was no longer thinking about it. He moved closer to me.

"Have you been a client of Altermann's for long?"

"No, I'm bringing him his newspaper," I replied earnestly.

He looked at me quite differently. Perhaps he knew about his lawyer's fantasy, or he might have had the same one. He carefully folded up *Le Monde* and handed it back to me. We looked at each other for a moment, then he put his hand on my thigh and, as I didn't say anything—I've never been the quickest with repartee—he kissed me on the mouth, as no one has ever kissed me before. Then he moved away and muttered:

"I'm so sorry."

"What for?"

Then he glanced at his watch and said that, if it was no inconvenience to me, his appointment could wait. I put the newspaper down on the sofa and we left. And then everything was different: I had pictured a bar, a Bloody Mary, perhaps some potato chips to make a change from the peanuts. . . . But no. It's true this man was well-known, he was in politics. I didn't know anything about it, but I pretended to. I even told him that I voted so as not to upset him. It was pouring rain—luckily because it meant no one saw us get into the back of his car, a long gray automobile with black windows. We traveled without saying a word to each other, his hand still on my thigh: it was like being in an aquarium of leather.

We came to a small street where the chauffeur opened the door for us and then drove the car away. We walked into a house as if it were our own, and he asked for a key. He told me to wait a minute and the woman sighed:

"That makes a full house now, a minor!"

I was far from being a minor, it's just it was dark and my hair was all over my face, and also I'm not very big, and not much has happened in my life. It's true that that preserves you. He came back very soon and took my hand, and we went into the most magnificent room, all red and gold, with a bed the size of my whole bedroom.

He didn't tell me that he loved me—he didn't have any reason to, mind you—but he made love to me like in the imaginary books you have inside your head. It was long, it was good, it was new, sometimes painful. We were more drenched than we had been in the rain and it was at about that stage that he gasped and begged me to come. I said: all right. And he collapsed on the bed, exhausted. Well, I really liked it. It made a change from the daily three minutes. He clutched my neck passionately and whispered that it was the first time he had come on his own and that it drove him crazy. I couldn't quite see the connection, so I told him that I was very happy too, but that I had to get back to the kiosk or my husband would start worrying. He looked at me, distraught; I could tell he didn't understand what I was saying.

"Can I see you again?" he asked.

"I don't know. I work."

He scribbled down a telephone number and asked me to hide it because it was his cell phone. I took the piece of paper as I dressed, and I kissed him one last time. He took some money from his jacket. I was surprised at first, and then I felt flattered: so I could pass for a professional? Incredible, especially from a man who was clearly used to call girls. I pushed the four 100 euros notes back toward him, saying I had learned a lot and that I should be the one paying. He smiled and said I was making fun of him: he was no fool, but he didn't dislike it.

"You didn't tell me your name," he said.

"Never the first time."

He looked at me with a sort of admiration which warmed me somewhere deep inside. I was even wetter than I had been earlier, when he had stared at me as he folded up *Le Monde*.

I closed the door quietly and went to catch the bus. When I reached the kiosk it had stopped raining. My husband was rolling back the plastic covers.

"You took your time."

I told him the elevator had broken down: I'd been stuck. He looked at me oddly, then snapped reproachfully, "Well, you can take the stairs next time."

"You can go next time," I said with a shrug, and I went back behind the magazines, amazed by the dishonesty I had mustered so naturally.

❦

It was only that night, lying back to back with my sleeping husband, that I thought of the politician again. Why had he begged me to come? No one had ever made any comment about it before. I shook my husband until he woke up.

"Do I usually come or not?"

"Of course you do," he grunted, half asleep.

I shook him a bit more.

"But how do you know? Is it something to do with me or do you compare me to the other women you've known?"

"Go to sleep," he said, stuffing his head under the pillow.

After an hour I was still not asleep, fizzing like a pinball. It was ridiculous, though: a politician who used prostitutes had taken me for a priceless call girl, and my husband couldn't even be bothered to tell me whether I came or not. I crawled from the bed over to the door and threw myself at the refrigerator. I stood there frantically gorging on pickles, salami, and jelly, swallowing down five slices of ham whole, licking the butter, and finishing with a swig from the bottle of cider before letting myself slide gently down the wall to sit on the floor. And then I thought of Charles Longereau, perhaps because he had a gray car too, and because he was the first man who had made me feel ashamed of being me.

I hadn't told my mother anything but I had known where he lived for the last five years. A lovely house covered in wisteria and honeysuckle, in the suburbs to the west. He didn't know me, so I could stay there for hours on Sundays, outside his house. That was before I was married; I didn't have the time now. And I had missed him since then. I had seen him five or six times coming out of the house to say goodbye to his children and his grandson. He kissed them affectionately and, when the car drew away, he would wave expansively. Before going back into the house he used to look up and down the street. Sometimes he would see me, but he never really looked at me. I was just a stranger passing by.

He would close the gate and I would stare at that dark green metalwork, and cry quietly, leaning against the wall opposite. I never dared approach him. I've always been afraid of disturbing people, but I was mostly afraid he would reject me once he met me. I preferred living in doubt. I told myself: if he had known me he would have loved me. My father would.

The following morning, in the harsh light of breakfast, Roger turned to me before taking his coat and said:

"What did you ask me last night?"

"Nothing," I replied, closing the garbage can.

Now I was the one getting up at five o'clock in the morning. My husband had trapped a nerve between two vertebrae, and the doctor had told him not to lift anything heavy while it recovered. He could have negotiated to have everything delivered on a temporary basis, but just the thought made him sick. So I told him: from tomorrow, I'll start the day. I took the returns back to Rungis and picked up the papers, then I opened the kiosk up at six thirty. My husband arrived at about eleven o'clock when I would go home to make lunch, then I would come back at about two when he would set off home again until he came to take over from me for the evening rush and to close up. We spent the whole time passing each other, switching this way and then switching back, until the day that he said, "Stop! We don't have a minute to ourselves anymore." I agreed, and he suggested that we go to see a marriage counselor. I opened my eyes wide and asked why.

"So that we can talk."

"And can't we just do that by ourselves?"

So Gisèle came and took over from us once a week, on Thursday afternoons. She didn't ask any questions. At first we stayed at home, slumped on the sofa, chatting. Well, it was mostly me talking. All he wanted to know was whether I had anything to tell him. I would ask him, "Do you find me attractive?" Things like that. He would say yes. I would pursue it, asking, "Did I come this morning?" And he would say, "Of course." It seemed so obvious to him that I didn't dare contradict him. So we ended up watching TV. Then his trapped nerve got back to where it was supposed to be and the doctor recommended walking and doing exercises to strengthen his spine.

"I'm going to do my exercises," he would say as he went out.

I offered to go with him three Thursdays in a row, but he wanted to be alone. I consoled myself by dialing the politician's number. As soon as he said hello, I would hang up. It felt good keeping someone waiting. I would see him again one day . . . maybe. Right then, it was Roger I missed. He still showed no interest in me, but everything was different now that I no longer felt responsible because another man had found me interesting. Sometimes I would imagine him coming home unexpectedly and we would make love for hours. But he never did. One day I wondered whether there was more to it than his back exercises. Perhaps, like me, my husband had another life going on inside his head. Perhaps he was more interesting than I thought. That was how the idea evolved, as I turned the pages of the men's magazines.

I bought a synthetic wig, really long and black, bright red lipstick, a pair of stiletto-heeled shoes, some seamed stockings, a black plastic raincoat that I could belt tightly at the waist, and some scent with a powerful smell of orchids that I found in a cheap shop. Even the butcher—I tried myself out on him—didn't recognize me. Judging by the way he looked at me, I'm pretty sure he would have given me the shoulder of lamb for free. But that wasn't the point: I was in training for the following Thursday.

IT FELT STRANGE SIDLING along the walls following my husband, given that I was so used to meeting him as we switched over. Every time he stopped I turned away quickly, afraid he would recognize me.

Then he suddenly walked into a movie theater. I remember thinking, I hope it isn't pornography. No, it was a war film. I hesitated before going in. What if he was meeting someone there? My heart was pounding but I wasn't there to trap him. What was I there for, then? I decided: Okay, if he is with someone, I'll come back out and go and drink a Bloody Mary.

I didn't buy the ticket out of jealousy, or curiosity, or a need to know whether my husband was going to the movies with someone else. No, I paid for my seat because it turned me on slipping into that darkened room, incognito. And with my every footstep these words kept ringing in my head: What do I look like in this outfit? It aroused me a good deal more than anything a man could have done to me. It gave me the same feeling I had when I was sixteen when Gisèle stole Mother Marie-Aimée's robes and, hunched over like the handle of an umbrella, I had walked out of the school through the teachers' door. I felt so free it burned deep inside me. And even more so on the way back when, with my pockets bulging with bubble gum, I went back into that prison for girls of my own free will.

I stood there for a long time unable to see anything, and then shadowy figures gradually emerged in the seats. There was hardly anyone there. I spotted him straight away, on his own, towards the back. Why go to the movies on his own when he had his home cinema in the apartment with me? In order to be on his own—I couldn't find any other explanation. He didn't want to be with me anymore.

I turned on my heel and walked back to the door, and then I reasoned with myself: It made no sense to go home and wait for him there. That wasn't *me*, that woman back there, the "perfect" woman he had locked me away in for his own peace of mind. And that wasn't *him* anymore either, that man who would come home that evening with a lie on his lips. A gratuitous lie: he wasn't doing any harm. Unless . . .

I went slowly back down the aisle. My new perfume was like a second skin. I had put too much of it on and it was going to my head, but he really mustn't recognize my smell. I hesitated: Should I sit a long way away from him or not? In the end I sat down just behind him. Shaking with fear, I brushed past him with my bag and said:

"I'm sorry," in a delicious accent I didn't know I had in me. I don't know whether it was the orchids but he replied in a voice I didn't know he had in him either, very distinguished, almost suave:

"It's quite all right, no harm done."

From behind he was another man. I noticed for the first time that his neck was powerful, his shoulders wide but his ears very delicate, and that he had a particular way of tilting his head.

Up on the screen Chinese men in old-fashioned costumes were massacring each other in slow motion, swiping their sabers in the moonlight, heads flying like soccer balls without a goal. When they weren't killing each other, they eyed each other in silence and the wind blew across the paddy fields, and the whole thing was magnificently boring. So I leaned toward the man who was my husband and I blew against his neck as I told him, although I have no idea why I said it, just to have something to say:

"That's my country."

He said, "Oh?" He wanted to turn around but I murmured to him not to move. He said that it was a beautiful country. I blew on his neck again, very gently at first, then harder, until I couldn't breathe anymore. He started moving his head, rolling it backward and forward on his shoulders. Then, languid and supple as a cat, he leaned his head on the back of the chair, with his eyes closed. I had never seen his face upside down. I was even more amazed by his reaction than by my own behavior. Did he like this sort of thing, then? Or was it because it was someone else doing it? I let my nose glide over his face, then I too closed my eyes and I kissed him on the mouth. With the most delicious feeling of guilt. His guilt.

But the screen suddenly went white and the lights came up. Terrified, I sat back in my seat and straightened my wig.

He said there was a problem with the reel, he wanted to stand up but I stopped him by putting my orchid-scented hands on his shoulders. Then I removed my hands; he didn't move. The room was darkened again and the film carried on.

"I love the way you smell," he said in a breathy whisper.

I smiled in the dark, but it wasn't a triumphant smile, it was one of those smiles that come as a reflex when you are about to cry. Then, very quietly, so that he wouldn't notice, I left the movie theater, all shaken up, with the same feeling of distress as someone coming away from a cemetery.

Back at the apartment, I stuffed the raincoat, shoes, stockings, wig, lipstick, and perfume into a plastic bag. I hid it at the bottom of the cleaning closet, which he never opens, and I took a long shower to get rid of the smell that my husband liked so much.

෴

He came home that evening with a beaming smile and announced:

"Get dressed. I have a surprise for you."

And he took me out to dinner to a Chinese restaurant. I couldn't get over it, couldn't swallow a single mouthful—mind you, it all kept falling off my chopsticks.

"Don't you like it?" he asked, so disappointed that it weighed on my heart.

"Yes, really. It's just hot."

I looked at his mouth nostalgically, thinking back to the afternoon. He had never kissed me so slowly and so hard. Even in the early days when he ran the kiosk with his brother and I used to come and buy a crossword book from him once a week and he would ask me if I'd done them all okay, and I would just say yes, not telling him they were for my mother and she never finished a single one because she insisted on thinking of herself as an "expert" like Gisèle's mother, then he admitted that he was more of a mental arithmetic man himself, as a hobby, and one evening he had tickets for the semi-final of a Math Society event called "Fun with Prime Numbers." He invited me to go with him and we had been together ever since. No, my heart had never beaten so hard as it did that afternoon at the movie theater. Perhaps because it wasn't me, it was a stranger who wasn't afraid of anything—not afraid of being shocking or being abandoned. So I asked him casually:

"Have you had a good day?"

He replied in his everyday voice, which had absolutely no effect on me:

"Not bad. I went to the movies. Actually, I've decided to go more often. The TV's bad for your eyes in the long run."

I suddenly felt sorry for him: he went to the movies because of his eyes. I was the one who had provoked him, I had kissed him by surprise. He just let it happen, but it could have been out of shyness. I almost told him the truth, then something stopped me. The image of him, from behind, with his head back . . .

"What about the movie? Was it any good?"

"A war movie. You would have liked it."

All at once he took my fingers in his hand. Hello, I thought, he knows it's me, he was just pretending. He leaned forward to smell my hand, then put it back down on the table.

"You smell of soap."

"Sure, I smell clean," I said, stupidly.

"Yup, that's right," he said with a kind of sadness I didn't know he had in him.

I was both relieved and disappointed. He had absolutely no inkling; he was just comparing me, and not to my advantage, either. He poured himself another glass of rosé wine, and then he talked to me about China, a country thousands of years old opening up to the world. I told him it was a long way away. He criticized me because I don't speak any other languages and I only like France. It made me think of my politician: I hadn't called him recently, not even to hang up straight away. Actually, he smelled clean, too. A smell of herbs from Provence. When it came down to it, I'd made love with a lavender bag, like in my mother's closet. I forced myself to finish my cold rice and my prawns in their congealed sauce. I felt quite light-headed, thinking: okay, so I'm eating out with my husband but I'm thinking about another man and he's thinking about another woman. At last we had found something we agreed on, and the whole idea turned me on so much that I forgot that my politician did actually exist.

When we got home my husband turned on the TV and offered me a beer.

"Yes, if you like."

I went to get undressed and came back in my baby-doll nightdress. He had given it to me as an anniversary present the year before. He looked at me without seeing me.

"Have you heard from my brother?"

"Why are you asking me about your brother?"

"No reason. Nevermind, it doesn't matter."

"Don't you like my nightdress any longer?"

"What's the connection?"

I stormed up and down the room, so angry it hurt.

"What *are* you doing?" he asked, sipping his beer.

"Nothing . . ."

"Well sit down and stop fidgeting about like that, you're making me dizzy."

I went and put on my flannelette nightdress, and came back to sit next to him in front of the TV. It was *ER*, like every Thursday. We drank our beer, but he didn't fall asleep. He suddenly took my hand without taking his eyes off the screen. I felt disarmed; maybe this was how he liked me, in my old nightdress. I watched him out of the corner of my eye, my heart pounding. And what if everything was about to change between us, now that he had almost cheated on me? As soon as the credits started to roll he stood up and I switched off the TV. He went to bed first. I brushed my teeth, taking my time over it, then I slipped into bed next to him as if it was the first time. When I turned over to switch the light off he put his hand over my buttocks, and I stayed there like that, all at an angle, quivering with desire. After a while his breathing became regular, his hand grew more and more limp and slipped back onto the sheet, and he started to snore.

I closed my eyes, thinking of Gisèle's long nails. And I tried to picture myself as a Chinese girl in the dreams going on next door.

It was the first Sunday of the month and, like the first Sunday of every month, we were going to have lunch with my mother.

On the second Sunday we went to have lunch with his parents.

On the third Sunday we went to have lunch with his brother, but that was before he left Gisèle; right now that had been substituted by the vegetarian restaurant that Gisèle took us to with her mother.

On the fourth Sunday we stayed at home because they all came to have lunch with us.

It's true that in the kitchen my mother is quite peerless (that's the sort of word they use in her crosswords) but after the *crudités* and a hot starter we have to have the main course with all the trimmings, then the salad complete with croutons to go with cheeses from the market—and not just any old market: cheeses straight from some isolated old farm up in the mountains, smelling of curdled milk or ewe's pee depending on the time of year—and then the homemade cake, usually a black forest gateau or a chocolate sponge. And with the coffee she produces *petit-fours* fresh from the oven, little almond fingers so soft you have to eat them piping hot or they harden straight away.

My husband, who gets up early even on a Sunday, then asks whether he can have a lie down on the sofa after we've had a glass of brandy. This gives my mother an opportunity to make sentimental remarks about this poor man exhausted by his work, and to carry on her monologue for the rest of the afternoon. Well, what's left of it.

"Look, he really does love you. Now, *he*'s someone who appreciates my cooking. You're very lucky, you know."

And I always say, "Yes. Thank you."

"And it means you're not on your own. Of course I'm not complaining: thank goodness I have you, both of you. I longed to have something of my own. A boy. Okay, so it didn't work out like that: I had a girl, it's not your fault, it's fate. I just had to think of a different name. But all the baby stuff, it just had to stay blue, you know. I couldn't afford to start again."

That last sentence had a reproachful ring to it. And on the first Sunday of every month, every time, I would hold my tongue while she went back over our past. I held my tongue to avoid conflicts. She was too old now to understand the hurt of never being able to call someone Dad—the only man who would have taken me in his arms with no designs to throw me down onto a bed.

But I never talked to her about my life. So she carried on talking to me about hers.

"The only thing I've ever got right on this earth is you. And I don't regret the sacrifices, you know. A child is the most fantastic thing that can happen to a woman, especially when she's on her own like me. Everyone said you were good enough to eat when you were little. I was so proud. They're absolutely right when they say a woman who hasn't had a baby isn't a real woman."

I looked at her, wondering whether she realized what she was saying, whether she was deliberately hurting me like this—given that, for now, I couldn't have children anymore.

And my first Sunday of the month trickled by without any confrontations between my snoozing husband and my mother, who never stopped congratulating herself for bringing me into the world.

Every time we left her apartment I had an overfull stomach and an empty heart . . . but my feelings of revolt petered out as I sat in the car with my seatbelt securely fastened. I would rest my head on my husband's shoulder and he would shrug me off sharply.

"Hey! Do you want us to crash?"

So I pressed my nose against the window and looked out at the River Seine, at the *bateaux-mouches*, the tour boats that I had never been on, and at the boarding around a building site that people called the Statue of Liberty, and I could see us falling into the water, amongst the dead fish, drowned forever in the sludge of the City of Light.

But this time when I rested my head on his shoulder he didn't push me away. Still concentrating on the traffic, he asked me:

"If you were cheating on me, would you tell me?"

I tried to think of an answer.

"Would you?" I asked.

He shrugged. And we sat there in silence with our question marks. After a while he said:

"Anyway, it's not an issue, is it?"

"No."

And I didn't know which of us we were talking about.

THE NEXT FEW DAYS PASSED painfully slowly. I didn't dare bring up the subject again. I couldn't check whether he felt any doubts about me or any remorse for kissing a stranger.

At last it was Thursday and he set out to the movies as if it was no big deal.

Trembling feverishly, I changed my shoes, belted my raincoat around my waist, and put on my black wig and my orchid scent. Then I looked at myself in the mirror. This girl wasn't really me. I didn't recognize myself. She didn't look like the girl I would have liked to be. She didn't mean anything to me. All I knew was that she was off to try and find a man in a movie theater, and that he too would be different. But he was still my husband, the man who had sworn before witnesses that he would be faithful to me, for better or for worse. The first man who really noticed me and who said "I want to share my life with you" one November evening in a little hotel room near Montparnasse station after the semifinal of "Fun with Prime Numbers."

Why does he no longer like the smell of my skin? I put on another spritz of orchid scent to drown my sadness. In the end I had found something; I did have an idea for an anniversary present.

It's not a war movie this week, but it's still part of the festival of Asian films. It's cheaper for the owner than showing new releases. He often comes and buys movie magazines from us, a funny little guy with very white skin who sighs when he thinks about having "exclusives," as he calls them. He always says that a local movie theater doesn't mean anything anymore. But he refuses to be bought out by the big names. He says he doesn't want to lose his soul.

On the poster for today's movie there are two very young Chinese girls outlined against bright sunlight and gazing at the ground.

I walk into the darkened theater as discreetly as possible but, like last time, there is hardly anyone there. There he is, I can see him, he's sitting in the same place, and I slip into the seat behind him. He turns his head slightly; he must have smelled my perfume. I smell him as I sit down. Oh, he's changed his aftershave, or he's put a bit of hair gel on. I move a little closer; no, it's the popcorn. He's wearing the shirt I ironed for him this morning. With a tie. He must have slipped that into his pocket before leaving, and tied it in the elevator to avoid any questions from me. I lean even closer. Oh no, it's the one he wore for our wedding! It's true, it is a nice one, but really . . . I shuffle back into my seat.

He's getting impatient. He spreads his arms and stretches them languidly along the backs of the chairs to either side of him. He leans his head back, staring at the ceiling. He looks so good like that, in the darkness, offered up.

I can't hold out any longer, and I whisper a little "Yi-hi" in his ear like the girls on the screen. "Yi-hi," he replies in a smoldering voice that could set the place on fire. Then, very slowly, I nibble his ear, move down his neck, ease open our tie, and, carefully, slide two fingers between the buttons of his immaculate shirt.

That is when he says, "*Wo aï ni,*" in flawless Chinese, just like they are saying it on the screen in front of me, subtitled with the words "I love you."

At the time I melted with pleasure, and then I remembered that he was saying "I love you" to another woman, even if it was his own wife, but he didn't know it.

I was so angry with myself I tore a button from his shirt and, as I left, I put on the most Chinese accent I could muster to say:

"Tomorrow, same time, same place."

Exactly the subtitles that were on the screen at the time, while the two girls smiled at each other discreetly, under the watchful eye of their foreman. And my husband didn't notice this because he had turned his back on them. I heard his seat creaking as he craned to watch me leave in the dark. I told myself: if he comes to tomorrow's rendezvous I'll leave him.

I WAS JEALOUS OF MYSELF. While I showered I rubbed myself, but with no enthusiasm. I thought of the two sexual experiences that had taught me so much: I could have done so many new things to my husband, but I was pretty sure that it wasn't with me that he wanted to do new stuff now.

While I waited for him I had made a nice meal and put on a pretty tablecloth—like my mother does. I had put on my makeup and a dress and shoes with heels nearly as high as those of the "other girl," and the whole time I kept fiddling with the button I had torn from his shirt.

He rang the bell, which he never does. I hid the button in a vase and opened the door for him, surprised but smiling.

"I must have lost my keys at the movies. It was so hot I took my jacket off, they must have fallen out."

"I'll go and see tomorrow, if you like," I wheedled. "Which theater was it?"

"Forget about it. I'll do it myself."

And he went off into the bedroom without even glancing at me, without seeing my pretty dress or the pretty table or anything. He came back in his shirtsleeves with his tie undone.

"It's been that kind of day. I even lost a button. Could you sew one back on?"

"I hope I'll be able to find one the same. Hey, you're wearing your tie from our wedding!"

He muttered that a tie was just a tie—it might as well be used. And he wandered off into the bathroom and yelled:

"Go ahead and eat, I'm not hungry this evening. I'm going to bed. Close the window, they've forecast a storm before morning."

I heard the water running, the sound of the toothbrush, the bedroom door. So I sat down, looked around the apartment and thought I would leave. Yup, I was making way for the "other woman," the one he was in love with. No, I wouldn't make a fuss. Yes, they could love each other without having to hide in some movie theater.

He came back into the living room.

"I'm thirsty. What are you doing all on your own, aren't you coming to bed?"

He took a beer from the kitchen and drank it straight from the bottle in front of me, watching me with a strange look in his eye.

"Are you talking to yourself now? What's happening to you, Nina?"

It was weeks since he had used my name. Months maybe. Those two syllables felt like a slap in the face.

"Nothing," I said. "You're the one who seems strange. You're the one who's changed."

"I've changed because you're not the same anymore. Okay?"

He came and stood squarely in front of me, pointing one finger at me and with his other hand on his hip. He looked ridiculous in his T-shirt and his checkered shorts.

"I don't know what's going on but ever since my brother left Gisèle I don't recognize you anymore."

"Will you stop talking about your brother! Why the hell does he have to keep coming between us?"

"The two of us were very close, don't you understand?"

"So? It's not my fault he dumped my friend!"

"Do you really not give a damn how much you hurt me? Why are you like this with me, Nina, why? This can't go on! I don't even exist anymore as far as you're concerned!"

I held his stare. He seemed to be utterly sincere, absolutely clear on the subject and sure he was right. He was the victim of an injustice. He was setting himself against me so that he had a reason to leave me, when I was actually just about to leave him. I felt like slapping him so that he would stop believing all these accusations about other people, but at the same time there was something touching about him, he was so fragile, at my mercy. Just one word about the festival of Asian films and he would be reduced to dust.

"Am I allowed to know what you're smiling about?" he asked tartly.

"I was thinking about tomorrow."

"What about it?"

I stared him right in the eye and that was when I grasped that if I left he would end up all on his own.

∞

I wake at twenty past five. My husband is in the shower and, for the first time since our wedding, he hasn't touched me. I realize that three minutes isn't much, but all the same . . . I'm used to it. I jump out of bed. I don't have any right to leave him like this; he is suffering, he is in a total dilemma, and it's my fault.

I hurl the bathroom door open, my mind made up.

"I have to tell you something, Roger. That girl with the black hair and the orchid scent, the girl in the row behind, it's me."

"I can't hear anything in the shower!" he replies, irritated.

I don't have the heart to tell him again. He is too tense, too on edge, and I feel more and more guilty. Guilty for insinuating my way into his head, guilty for turning him on and deriving so much pleasure from it. He's right: I have changed with him. I am torturing him. After all, I did cheat on him first. And he can tell, even if he is afraid to admit the truth to himself, that's all.

The only thing to do is to stop going to the movies. That woman no longer exists. We will forget about her.

"Is the coffee ready?"

He knots his towel around his waist and brushes right past me, pushing me slightly to get out, without even noticing that I'm half naked.

I have made the coffee, and I have put our two blue coffee cups on their two blue saucers, planted the little wooden knife into the butter, toasted the bread and taken the lids off the honey and the jam. As usual. As I put the four sugars into his coffee I feel that those four sugars are as far as our complicity goes today, and I know for sure that he is going to leave me. I run over to the bedroom to tell him the truth again, but when I hear him speaking I stop. I open the door gently.

"*Ni hao wo jiao Roger.*"

He's speaking Chinese? But who to? "She" didn't give him a phone number for goodness sake. No, he has earphones on, and he's repeating:

"*Ni hao wo jiao Roger.* Hello, my name is Roger."

Fourth Sunday in the month: everyone has come to lunch. Thirty-five plates, sixty-four pieces of cutlery, twenty-one glasses, plus the dishes, saucepans, and casseroles and the broken-down dishwasher. The cheese soufflé went wrong, the leg of lamb was overcooked, and the potatoes stuck to the pan and turned to mush. I felt so ashamed I just spent my time running back and forth to the kitchen. When I finally brought in the dessert, which my mother had made, everyone was in raptures about the wonderful chocolate charlotte, and they went on to talk about the signature dishes of various restaurants they knew, where everything was so delicious and rarified. My husband was the only one not saying anything. He wasn't eating either. No one had come to join him at the cinema on Friday and he was sulking with me—not realizing how justified that was.

I wasn't feeling too good either. I felt lonely, I could see he was unhappy, and I thought: what's the point. In order to get away on Friday he invented an appointment with the osteopath, and he came back half an hour later saying he had got the wrong day. Which left him with a pretext he could use again for the next assignation. That was what hurt me the most: that stinginess, the lack of effort he put into finding an excuse. I could imagine him trying to find an answer in the mirror, looking at himself with a mixture of pride, anxiety, and bafflement: Why had she chosen him? Would he have any chance of appealing to her by the light of day, in all the stupidity of his everyday life, in the middle of his kiosk? I could feel the trouble he went to trying to imagine the life this girl led outside the movie theater, and I found that touching in spite of myself. Was I an illegal immigrant? Or a diplomat's wife who came to soothe her homesickness during the festival of Asian films. "You're not yourself," my mother had commented with the second failed dish.

When I came back from the kitchen having cleared the table, she was playing cards with Henriette, Gisèle's mother, and my mother-in-law was putting on her coat.

"Roger's taking us to the movies."

I started to shake from head to foot. He had no right to bring his family into this.

"What are you going to see?" I asked, trying to smile and sound as natural as possible.

"The one I saw on Thursday. I'm sure they'll like it."

"I'll come with you," Gisèle decided.

"And why don't you come with us?" my mother-in-law asked, surprised.

"I don't like the movies."

"To each his own," my husband said conclusively, putting on his jacket.

My mother retorted that I used to like it *before*. Gisèle said there was nothing unusual about that: we always end up loathing what we've adored.

"You may," my mother replied, "but I never change my mind. I'm not a flibbertigibbet."

My husband went out with a shrug of his shoulders. My mother-in-law asked again whether I would like to go with them, but her husband dragged her out onto the landing with a firm but gentle hand, as if to say: let people get on with their own lives. It was Gisèle who slammed the door.

"You could make a bit of an effort, for goodness sake," my mother told me, "and go to the movies when your husband asks you to."

"He wasn't the one who asked me. It was his mother."

"All the more reason, then. If he divorces you one day, you'll know why. Well, do what you like. Are you going to play with us? Henriette would like it."

Henriette smiled kindly to let me know that I really didn't have to. She was exactly the opposite of my mother: self-effacing, discreet, quiet with her unhappiness. And exactly the opposite of Gisèle. Gisèle treated her with a mixture of exclusive passion and unfair cruelty, to which she responded with even-handed gentleness.

"No, thank you," I said, smiling at her. "I have to do the dishes."

My mother raised her eyes to the heavens saying I always had an excuse for everything.

"It's not an excuse. The dishwasher's broken."

"Well, when does that machine ever work?"

"When I'm on my own."

And I went off into the kitchen.

With that she complained to Henriette that I was aggressive and that I neglected my appearance. She thought I was weird, and she had been wondering for a while whether I was actually her daughter. She had read in the paper that they sometimes made mistakes with the tags in maternity wards.

"And also, the first word she said, when she was thirteen months old, was 'Daddy.' To some guy who came to repair the TV. I've never forgotten that: it gave me such a shock . . ."

"It's easier to say 'Daddy' than 'Mummy,'" Henriette replied kindly.

"Except she didn't have anyone to say it to! It was just to spite me, to belittle me in front of a repairman!"

Now, I'm normally very calm with my mother, but I burst out of the kitchen yelling that the dishes could wait and I was going out to get some air. Before leaving I took the plastic bag with my wig, perfume, and movie clothes. And there, in the hallway, everything suddenly started spinning. I hung onto the radiator and closed my eyes. I heard my mother explaining how hard it was having a girl. And not a boy. Boys always stayed tied to their mother's apron strings. They're always their little babies. Henriette was trying to get a word in, just to say she understood, given that she too had a girl . . . but my mother cut her off with a definitive:

"Yes, but I brought mine up on my own."

There was a silence like someone had just been hanged. I opened my eyes again. My mother was shuffling the cards.

"What did your husband die of again?"

"But he didn't die," Henriette protested timidly. "He's in a home."

"Are you sure?"

"Oh yes," Henriette replied with a long sigh.

"That's my daughter's fault again. Sometimes she talks so quickly and so quietly, I just catch the occasional word, and that's the result. She'll have to apologize to you."

Henriette said it didn't matter, given the state her husband was in. Then, in a good loud slow voice, she explained that she had kept him at home as long as she could, right up to the day when he picked up a Swiss knife and tried to chop her up because he thought she was a free-range chicken. And she was such a tiny little thing. At first the doctors thought it was a temporary lapse, maybe a marital crisis, but they gradually started talking about schizophrenia.

"Well, if we had to take the doctors' word for it, we'd all be locked up," my mother announced. "I don't need to get people confused with free-range chickens to want to murder them. It's your turn."

Their words were spinning around me and I could feel a great lump in my chest. Schizophrenia, marital crisis, Swiss knife . . .

"And he was such a calm man," Henriette went on.

I was calm too. I didn't say anything either. Every time I had tried to confide in my mother, all through my childhood, she had said, "That's enough problems for today." Problems belonged at the medicaid office: she listened to complaints and reasoned with dissatisfied people from nine till five. She wanted a bit of peace at home. That was how I ended up at boarding school. I told myself it would be all right once she retired, but she had stayed the same, just without the counter to sit behind.

"Enough talking. Let's play!"

Henriette opened a little box she had put on the table, and took a tablet.

"I hope that isn't mint candy, because if you're taking homeopathic remedies, they'll have no effect."

"No, it's for my heart."

"Oh good," said my mother. "It's your turn to take a card." Then she caught sight of me on the doorstep and added, "I thought you'd gone. Well, go on then, go and get your fresh air!"

She had never listened to me. My husband didn't see me anymore. When it came down to it the only time I wasn't alone was when I became the other woman. The one who had no past, no connections, no obligations. The one who didn't feel any disappointment or injustice. The one who fueled someone's dreams.

WHEN I REACHED THE MOVIE theater I hesitated. Who should I go in as? Me or the *other?*

The guy selling tickets didn't even look up when he told me the movie had already started. I told him it didn't matter because I'd already seen it. I paid and stepped into the darkness, carrying the *other* at arm's length in her plastic bag. The four of them were sitting in a row toward the middle. I nipped over to sit down next to my husband who was near the end of the row.

"Okay?" I whispered, feeling intimidated now that I was there as myself.

"Why are you here?" he asked through clenched teeth.

"So that I can spend Sunday with you," I said very tenderly. "To show you I haven't changed."

He didn't react. After a few minutes he risked glancing over toward the door. I put my hand gently on his arm and moved my leg next to his, but he snapped away. So I sat there hugging my plastic bag to me.

A young girl with long dark hair stood up from her seat. I saw her the same moment my husband did. She passed in front of us, supple and feline, and knocked my knee so that I dropped the plastic bag. The orchid scent released from it enveloped her as she moved through it. My husband gave a start. His whole body strained toward her, motionless, and in that moment I realized how much he wanted her and how much he was having to restrain himself because of me. It had a profound effect on me: I had never been so aware of existing for him.

She suddenly came to a stop. I stopped breathing. She retraced her steps, passed in front of the screen and leaned over, with her long hair obscuring her face, to pick up the umbrella she had left on her seat, then she went out by the other door to avoid disturbing the same people three times.

My husband leaped to his feet. After treading on my foot without even realizing it, he went out too. Without think-ing, I picked up my bag and ran after him much to the an-noyance of Gisèle, who said that if we didn't like it we could at least let other people watch it.

I wasn't unhappy, no; I was hurt that he could get me confused with a stranger. I had to talk to him, to tell him the truth: that's not her, that's someone else who has nothing to do with us.

But once outside I saw him looking right and left, com-pletely lost: she had disappeared. He sat down on a bench with his arms spread along the backrest, leaning his head back, like on the day we first kissed. And I wanted him so badly. I so badly wanted to make love to this man without him recognizing me. To meet a second time, but as we were in real life, deep down inside us, free and new, without the childhood problems, without the fears and the inhibitions that had turned us into this pathetic little couple, this pair of strangers. But now wasn't the time. It was Sunday, family, obligations, pretenses. We had plenty of time to ourselves. I thought that, for now, I should leave him alone with his disappointment.

As he hadn't seen me come out of the movie, I went back in.

When I sat down Gisèle kept asking me what was going on so I told her to shut up. Pretty harshly, I admit. I must have looked at the images on the screen for two minutes, and then I closed my eyes. When the lights came back up Gisèle was pointing her finger right under my nose and whispering so that my parents-in-law couldn't hear:

"I don't know what's going on with your husband, but he's behaving exactly like his brother. If you don't lay off him a bit, you can kiss your marriage good-bye."

She was wagging her finger in front of my mouth; I bit it. She stifled a scream, and I left with my plastic bag. My husband was still on his bench. I told him I would walk home while he ran his parents back to Malakoff.

"Why, what's the matter with you?"

"I'm not married to them, and you're not married to my mother. Don't we have a right to spend Sunday together just the two of us sometimes? I'm fed up with having them at our throats the whole bloody time!"

He muttered through his teeth to tell me to be quiet, went back to his parents, and led them over to the parking lot without a glance in my direction. Gisèle took me to one side and told me I wouldn't solve my problems by being aggressive. I had only one friend and if I started biting her when she was giving me sound advice, then there wasn't much point hoping she would pick me up when I wound up on my own. I told her I hadn't had my vaccinations and she had better go and have a tetanus injection. She turned on her heel, digging out her cell phone to call her doctor. I couldn't stand the people I loved anymore, and it wasn't their fault. I was sabotaging my own life and it was better that way. I looked at my plastic bag and automatically eased my grip on it, as if to let the other woman breathe.

ᘓᵐᵐᕲ

As I walked home I could feel my decision hardening with every footstep: I would leave, disappear. And come back one day as the *other*, perhaps I would become her for good.

With the traffic jams, I had an hour ahead of me before Roger came back from Malakoff. Turn out my mother and Henriette, pack a suitcase, leave a note. I composed it in my head as I walked along those walls I wouldn't be seeing anymore. I explained, justified, ratified: all that was left was "I'm going." I would go wherever I happened to go, somewhere, anywhere.

But then nothing happened the way it was supposed to. When I opened the door I found my mother in the most terrible state. Henriette was sitting on her chair, leaning back with her head bent over her cards.

"Here's the problem: you don't have a cell phone, I can never get hold of you! And I've called my doctor but his answering machine was on!"

I told her to calm down and I took Henriette's pulse. I was sad because I was fond of her and at the same time I was thinking: this is just like her—leaving like that, discreetly, with no fuss or explanations, and no complaining. My mother picked up the whisky bottle and poured herself half a glass.

"Are you going to drink all that?"

"Would you rather I had a heart attack, too? Who are you calling?"

"Gisèle, on her cell phone."

"Some people have all the luck."

⌒〰〰⌒

They all arrived at the same time. Gisèle ran over to her mother to put her arms around her, and in her enthusiasm she toppled her off her chair. My husband's parents gasped in terror and my mother, who was onto her third whisky, said:

"I'm not feeling too good."

Gisèle stayed there with her mouth open, not a single sound had come out of it. And then everyone started talking at once, flapping around Henriette. There were those who wanted to sit her back up, and those who thought it better not to move her. I didn't think anything: I listened and responded but I was no longer there.

"We need to tell the undertakers," my husband decided.

"The council!" my father-in-law corrected. "This is their department."

I reminded them it was Sunday.

"The church," my mother-in-law suggested.

"Never!" Gisèle replied, her eyes vacant. "Let's call a doctor!"

I looked at Henriette and tried to pray for her soul but it was hard: the nuns had ruined God for me. I wondered where she was now, whether she could see us or whether she had already drawn a line under all this, forgotten everything about her former life, just as I had decided to do half an hour earlier. I told myself I had made my decision and that it was still valid. At the same time I had lost the momentum: would I still have the courage to do it?

My husband had made some coffee and was handing it around. As he passed me he squeezed my shoulder, and I suddenly felt pathetic. I could picture him moving heaven and earth trying to find out where I had gone to, and I suddenly wanted to come back.

When the doctor arrived my mother, who was lying full length on the sofa with three cushions under her feet, groaned and said:

"Oh! doctor, you're here!"

She held out her arm for him to take her blood pressure. We let her get on with it because she was very pale and we already had one dead body. He looked baffled and tapped the gauge a few times, then released the arm band and said reassuringly:

"You've almost got the blood pressure of a young girl."

"Why *almost*?" replied my mother, grabbing his sleeve with unexpected force. "You can tell me the truth: I have a previous history . . ."

"Mom, he's here for Henriette."

She pinched her lips, and he was free to declare the death. We helped him lie the body down on the sofa, asking my mother to make room for us. He told us we should contact the undertakers, but that we could keep Henriette until the following morning because it was Sunday. I told him that this wasn't her home, and he said it didn't matter but that we weren't allowed to move her. Just before he left he patted my mother's hand and murmured:

"Have a nip of whisky, it will pick you up. You've had quite a shock, it's absolutely normal."

My mother fluttered her eyelashes and looked deep into his eyes with the Mona Lisa smile she reserved for medics.

"I'll see you to the door, doctor. Could I have your cell phone number?"

⁂

We put Henriette on our bed. Gisèle felt it was more decent, for a funeral vigil. Roger surrendered our room without a word. He just whispered that, given the situation, he would stay over with his parents. I nodded, as if I understood, as if it didn't matter to me, as if I thought it was quite normal for him to leave me alone at a time like that.

When they had left I shut myself in the kitchen to do the washing up. I didn't know whether I was still going to leave, but I would make sure everything was left tidy. With every plate, images of Henriette loomed in front of me, the picnics we used to have when she used to take us out of boarding school, once a month on a Sunday, in her little white Fiat. Her yogurt cup, she used to call it. With our hair buffeted by the wind or soaked with rain through the holes in the roof, Gisèle and I were almost happy. Her job made us laugh: she was a lingerie rep for Paris and its suburbs, and she always had hundreds of anecdotes that were too adult for us and that we couldn't wait to repeat in the dormitory. We would eat sheltering in a barn or on a plaid rug spread out on the grass beside a river. She would gorge us with cold meats and coffee-flavored éclairs washed down with sparkling wine, and it would be our secret. On the other Sundays, when she came with her husband or my mother, it would be serious restaurant, fish full of bones, mineral water, white napkins, and "sit up straight." I cried over my sink full of lemon Joy. I suddenly realized the fact that I had lost Henriette because I was alone in my kitchen and there was nothing I could do for her now. She wasn't that body laid out on my bed, all stiff and cold and watched over by her daughter. She was my Sunday fairy godmother in her yogurt cup, with her hams and her cheap bubbly.

I went back to the living room, my mother was sitting in a chair sobbing. I put my hand on her shoulder and she squeezed my fingers. It felt good to be sharing the same pain.

"When I think it could be me in there, on your bed . . ."

I took my hand away.

"In the meantime, it's her, Mom. She was your friend. Don't you think you should go and say good-bye to her?"

She sat bolt upright:

"Surely you're not going to resent me for being alive!"

"I don't hold anything against you. I'd just like it if this hurt you a little more, that's all."

"Who are you talking to about pain? I get palpitations if the least thing upsets me, I have to take on so much . . ."

I didn't say anything in reply, I just offered to take her home so that she could get some sleep.

"I'll have plenty of time to sleep when I'm on the other side."

"But you're not on the other side!" I screamed unexpectedly, shaking her by the shoulders. "I don't give a damn about your palpitations, there's nothing wrong with you, you don't even have a heart, all you can feel is self-pity! The only use she was to you was to play cards! And what about me, what use am I to you? Mmm?"

The telephone stopped me from saying anymore. It was my brother-in-law who had just called Malakoff and couldn't understand why Roger had hung up on him. I did the same thing, unplugged the phone, and then went to heat up the coffee.

When I got back my mother had taken up her position on the sofa again with her shoes off and her feet planted on top of the three cushions. I could see straight away that this was how she intended to spend the night. As if I hadn't said anything, as if she was being good enough not to respond to words that I would regret in the morning.

I went to take some coffee to Gisèle, who was prostrated in a chair that she had drawn up to the bed. I sat down next to her and stroked her hair as you would a child's. She squeezed my hand very hard. She was one of those people who screamed and ranted at the least provocation, and she seemed so calm now that it almost frightened me. We stayed there, without moving, watching her mother who wasn't moving either, her head with its permed hair perfectly central on the pillow. Three silent lonely figures.

"Is it easier when you believe in God?"

I said I didn't know.

After a while, Gisèle asked me if I had a blanket.

"Are you cold?"

"No, it's for her. She's always felt the cold."

The blanket was under the bedcover, underneath her mother. I went to get my down jacket and did my best to cover Henriette with it, as she lay there with her fingers crossed over her stomach like someone who has just finished a large meal. When I put her there I had joined her hands as if in prayer, but Gisèle had rectified that. I sat back down.

She shook her head, staring at the body, which was lent an air of hope by my warm pink jacket.

She suddenly turned toward me and said rather anxiously:

"She could be you."

I looked at Henriette and thought about my life. Perhaps it wasn't too late for everything.

"Where are you going?"

"I'll be back."

I TOOK THE TRAIN OUT TO Vésinet-Centre. It was now or never. There was some significance to that "She could be you," coming to Gisèle just like that. It wasn't by chance. That's what I kept telling myself to try to convince myself as I was rocked by the night train sandwiched between kids in earphones and vacant-looking people who lived in the suburbs.

I walked through the sleeping streets, past the gates that keep the dogs in. It had stopped raining. The lights were on in about a third of the houses, TVs flickering, dispensing gunfire, shouts, or laughter. I went from one station to the next as I hurried past. It was now or never. I was scared to death, clenching my teeth, shaking and repeating the words "I don't know who I am anymore" to give me courage. Not Roger's wife or the Chinese girl of his dreams. I don't want to be either of them anymore. I want something new, to be the person I should have been from the start, my father's daughter.

There was only one light on in the house behind the green gate. On the first floor, on the right. Perhaps it was an office. He works late, he has his own business, he brings files home. I rang the bell and it made a peeling sound like the Christmas bells outside a department store. Twelve dogs barked, all around. It's me, Daddy.

After a while someone opened the door, and through the bars I could see a woman with her hair in a bun. His wife. The mother I could have had if she had gone to the treatment spa with him in Néris-les-Bains instead of letting him go off on his own to meet a stranger. But it's him I look like. I've been told that ever since I was little: "She's exactly like you"—the sentence my mother repeated so lovingly to the glass frame on the sideboard. And the variation she addressed to me when I caught them in the middle of one of their silent conversations: "He would recognize you straight away."

"Is there someone there?"

I hid behind the wisteria. The woman asked her question again, harshly, not moving. What could I tell her? "Good evening. I'm so sorry to disturb you. Is your husband there? I'm your stepdaughter." I had been so sure that he would open the door, that it would be *him*. That the courage I had shown was a calling, that the time had come, that the scene I had always dreamed of would finally unfold. But it wasn't meant to be a scene for three people.

"Go and play somewhere else and leave people in peace!"

She closed the door. I stared at that first-floor window, hoping that he would at least show himself, that he would come to see what was going on. For years, at boarding school, I had written him letters and kept them in the bottom of a large envelope marked "To be opened after my death." I've never read them since. I grew up thinking they could be for my children.

I know we shouldn't go backward. But it's the only way I can move forward.

I headed back to the station with my father still intact in the bottom of my heart, just one more missed opportunity, one part of me that still hadn't started and that was now my only hope. At least I hadn't ruined any of that side of things. Everything was still possible.

It would have to wait until another time.

THE MOMENT WE WALKED into the shop the man sat us down in front of a varnished desk and gave us the sort of relaxed smile you would expect of someone selling sofas.

"It's for her mother," I said tactfully.

"I understand. My deepest sympathy."

He took out a catalogue. It felt strange, it was just like being back with Gisèle three years earlier, talking to the same sort of man, drawing up our wedding lists. I missed Roger, terribly. Not the Roger he had become. The night I had just spent without him had erased the last few weeks. I couldn't believe that he would go on being this stranger in love with a stranger. We deserved a second chance, he and I.

"Right. Well, we'll proceed by a process of elimination. Are we looking at the top of the range? Solid oak is still . . ."

I cut him off, murmuring that the person in question wanted to be cremated.

"I understand. No oak."

"Why not?" Gisèle protested. "If that's the best there is . . . I'm not going to skimp on the price. Mom has always been generous."

"It's not a question of price," the salesman said with discreet sort of smile. "We'll come back to that."

He stood up and we watched him go over to an urn that was a good meter tall and looked like an Egyptian casket.

"This one is very popular. It's quite unusual, but it all depends on what you're going to do with it. The interior design aspect isn't such a taboo anymore. In fact there's quite a trend for integrating them into their surroundings. The little vase hidden in a bedside table or shut up in a shoe box has had its day."

Gisèle leaned toward me and whispered, "She'd be lost in there."

"Don't you have something a bit more intimate?" I asked. "I mean, not so spacious?"

He went over to another design, more like a candy jar.

"Oh no!" Gisèle responded straight away. "She'd never get into . . ."

So he picked up a pretty piece in Sèvres porcelain.

"Yes, that one!" said Gisèle. "It's her favorite color, emerald green."

"How much is it?" I asked discreetly.

Gisèle's cell phone rang.

"A hundred and fifty euros excluding taxes."

"I'll pay for this," I muttered quickly, glancing at Gisèle.

"It's a very beautiful gift, you won't regret it. Right, shall we consider the coffin?"

"It's not worth it: she's being cremated."

"You will still need a coffin. They're not going to throw her into the flames with their bare hands," he added with a sympathetic little smile, as if he thought I didn't understand.

"I'm so sorry."

"It's not unusual. This is the first time, I imagine."

"Yes. Well . . . for cremation, yes."

He explained that the problem with oak was that it burned very slowly and went on for hours after the funeral ceremony which most people found upsetting. But, on the other hand, there were others who wanted it to go on as long as possible. It was obviously in his interests to persuade us in favour of the oak, he said, but in these circumstances profit had to bow before human kindness, didn't it? Particularly as there wasn't a huge difference in price—I gathered that much from his catalogue when I saw the rates for pine, which charged very highly for its speedy combustion.

"As far as the urn is concerned, have we made the right choice? It's not too big is it?"

He looked at me with a mixture of indulgence and gratitude, because I was taking all this to heart. In fact, I felt outside the whole experience, I felt cold and pointless, like all those times my mother trailed me to various cemeteries. "Say good-bye to your grandmother, throw a handful of soil over her, it will bring her good luck." "Your godmother was such a pretty woman and she loved you so much." "Look, your grandfather didn't make it." "Say a prayer for cousin Jeanne." Those big wooden boxes lowered gently into the ground. I can vaguely remember the faces of the men holding the ropes. Strangers. Who didn't even cry.

My hair was always done immaculately, my clothes brand new. My mother took hours getting me ready so that I would be a credit to her. "Your daughter's so pretty and good and well behaved . . ." With every death she took her revenge on life. And I was like those young heiresses with their awkward expressions, the ones she showed me in her magazines, heading off to the debutante balls. "They're making their entry into the world," she told me proudly. My entry into the world happened in cemeteries, about two or three times a year. A large family is a terrible thing—if they are all old. You spend your whole time being more alone. Time goes by and you never really grow up. You cling to the last few, even if they aren't worth the effort, because you already feel guilty for outliving them, and you haven't even had children to keep up the ritual.

"It's an excellent choice."

I came back down to earth. He was talking about the urn. Actually, this was the first time I had taken responsibility for funeral arrangements. The little girl with the walk-on part at the cemetery had given way to a grown-up who was about to write a check.

"In any event," he went on, "it's better to overestimate. They don't just put the person's ashes in. There's the wood too, of course . . . I mean, they're not going to sift through it."

He said this in a voice laden with regret. I looked at him and nodded. If he had been selling sofas, I would have found him quite good-looking. He asked me for my address, and I hesitated, glancing at my friend who was out on the sidewalk on the phone. He explained that it was to send me the bill, which would come to around 2,135 euros inclusive of taxes. Confronted with my blank expression, he told me again that I wouldn't regret it, and that he would take care of all the formalities.

That was when Gisèle came back. It was her aunt who had called from Alsace: she couldn't get away for the cremation—and, anyway, she and her sister didn't talk to each other anymore, they hadn't for four years, but she would be with us in spirit at the crematorium, and she would be expecting us in Strasbourg to put Henriette in the family grave.

Gisèle asked the salesman whether it was possible, after the cremation, to wrap up the urn with plenty of padding so that it wouldn't break, because she wasn't yet sure whether she would take the train or entrust it to a courier company. After all, she had fallen out with her aunt too, in her mother's memory.

WHEN I GOT BACK THE KIOSK was closed. I couldn't believe it: Roger had stayed with his parents and was leaving me to cope on my own. Surely he didn't think I was going to get on with everything at the same time—the funeral arrangements, the undertakers, and the kiosk?

I stormed home and found him standing in the kitchen watching the round window of the washing machine.

"Have you put a wash in?" I asked.

I couldn't get over it: it was the first time since I had known him. He explained that he didn't want to sleep in sheets that smelled like a morgue. I was paralyzed, quite unable to ask him the question that was eating at me: had he used the fabric softener?

"Right, I'm going to open up the kiosk. We need to speak this evening."

He walked around me to get out of the kitchen.

"Roger?"

He turned around; I swallowed hard and gathered all my courage.

"What?"

"Did you put the Snuggle in?"

"Is that it?"

He slammed the front door and I stayed there, still rooted to the spot, not knowing whether his aggression was to do with Henriette's sheets or the fact that he had discovered the plastic bag. At the back of the cupboard, behind the bottle of fabric softener, I had been hiding the woman of his dreams.

I ran to the door and caught up with him on the landing just as he was stepping into the elevator.

"What do you want to talk to me about, Roger?"

"This evening."

"Why not now? There's no rush to get there now."

He hesitated, then nodded and let go of the elevator door. He went back to the kitchen and poured himself a glass of water which he drank down in three gulps, staring over toward the sink. Then he turned to face me and, with his arms hanging by his sides, he drew in his breath as if about to pick up one of our piles of newspapers, but he sat down.

"All right. Let's talk."

I pulled out the chair opposite him, nice and slowly. The noise of the washing machine started up again, churning through the silence.

"How long has this been going on, Nina?"

A shiver ran down from the nape of my neck. I tried to put more amazement than distress into my "What?"

"You know exactly what I'm talking about. How long has it been going on?"

"But what do you mean?"

"My brother and you."

I sat there with my mouth gaping.

"There's no point denying it. I'm not blind. I can see you've changed. Your pubic hair trimmed into a little heart, your nightdress snipped up with scissors, wanting to suck me off, questions about orgasms . . . He's introduced you to different stuff, has he? And you want the rest of the family to benefit from it."

I was so taken aback that I hardly even protested as if he was going too far.

"I said there's no point denying it! When I helped him move I found your blue dress in his things. What do you say to that? That you lent it to Gisèle and he forgot to give it back to her when he dumped her? That's what he said."

I spread my hands helplessly. He was taking the words out of my mouth. He raised his voice to stop my interrupting.

"He and I have never lied to each other in our lives! Stop looking at me like that! He had that same look, all innocent and shocked and goddamn two-faced. You make me sick! How long's it been going on? Mmm? Tell me!"

I hesitated for a moment, as if I was about to name a date, and then I said:

"I don't know why you've got this into your head, but I swear to you I'm not cheating on you with your brother!"

The ring of truth in my voice threw him. Then he shrugged his shoulders and sniggered rather sadly.

"It's already over, is that it? You get him to leave his wife, then you dump him, just for the fun of destroying something. Who the hell are you, Nina? Who are you?"

The spin cycle made me jump. I stood up and went to take him in my arms but he shoved me back, knocking his chair over in the process, and he turned his back on me. He stood looking out the window with his hands in his pockets, listing all the details in my behavior that had led him to uncover what he called the "the terrible truth." I didn't recognize any of the thoughts he attributed to me, as if he had been living with someone else for weeks. However much I told myself he was only trying to justify his attraction to the Chinese girl and his own desire to leave me, I was devastated by the accumulated suffering in his silences, his observations and deductions. And there I was thinking he didn't notice me anymore. He had clocked every word, every look, every gesture, and he had an interpretation for everything.

I waited till he had finished speaking, then I took him over to the telephone, dialed his brother's number, and handed him the other handset. For five minutes Roger listened to us swearing the same thing, protesting our innocence and the complete indifference we felt for each other.

"So I'm an asshole, then?" he concluded.

And he hung up. He dropped down onto the sofa, completely dazed. He believed us, and that took a weight off his shoulders, but it created a void.

"Why have you become like this with me, then, if there's nothing between you?"

I came and sat on the floor at his feet, and hugged his knees. I told him gently that he wasn't the same either, but people had every right to change, to evolve, and that didn't mean they had to lose each other along the way.

"It's because we didn't have any children, that's all."

I gulped: he had spoken in the past tense without thinking about it, so automatically that it hurt me. I almost told him my little secret, the reason I might never be able to conceive again, but he suddenly stood up, his face set stubbornly:

"Maybe we're just not meant to be together."

I held him back. I said that, if he agreed to it, we could go for a consultation at the hospital the very next day to see if we could undergo treatment. At least it would give us something to aim for. And I was completely sincere: I knew that if he wanted it, as I did, this child would come and save us.

He looked at me sadly, and said with a sort of resignation:

"I'm talking love and you give me hospitals."

Then he looked at the clock. He started to head for the door, but turned around.

"I'm sorry, about my brother. But in a way it would have been more simple. I can't stand lies. But not understanding is even worse . . . with a couple everything's meant to be clear. Otherwise the relationship doesn't mean a thing, and we're not a couple anymore and I just can't . . ."

I let the door close behind him. What else could I do? Give him some justification for all his suspicions? Own up to Monsieur Jean and the politician? Maybe he would own up to the Chinese girl in exchange. Maybe he would elaborate

on it, inventing a real affair, to make us even, and then everything would be possible for us once more. We would set off
on track again, with a bit of extra baggage, but it would be
the same track. Ours.

Was that what I wanted?

My mother opened the door as soon as I rang. She had asked to see me urgently. I thought it was because of what I had dealt her on Sunday: I was ready to confront her sulking, recriminations, and emotional blackmail. She asked me if I was feeling better, if I wasn't so tired. She knew I had cracked under the strain, that I had spoken impulsively, without thinking, it wasn't my fault and she wouldn't hold it against me—it was forgotten. I looked away: she would never hear what was weighing on my heart, it was too late. She gave me a knowing smile:

"Have you brought me a little something to make me forgive you?"

"No."

I was holding the other woman in my hand, in her plastic bag. I didn't want to leave her alone at the apartment, to run the risk of Roger finding her, not in the state he was in.

"Sit down."

She seemed very agitated, and told me she had had a horrible feeling of foreboding since the morning.

"I've been thinking," she said, "what happened to Henriette is a warning. We never worry about the people we love when we should. Call your father, please."

She played this one on me every six months or so, to set her mind at rest. I had to put on a different voice each time, to pass myself off as Interflora, the post office, or some kitchen company. She didn't want to disturb anyone, she had never let him know how she was or about me—she wasn't going to tell him he had a daughter now, I mean not at his age. All she had ever agreed to tell me was that he was a very good man who had nothing to feel guilty about, and that his wife was a good woman too, and that a little slip up between two adults at a treatment spa had no right to ruin two lives—she didn't mean ours. No, she just wanted to know how he was. He never answered the phone, but she always had the same palpitations, staring at the loudspeaker on the phone, her fingers clutching my shoulder, while I asked the wife, the secretary, or the son whether I could speak to Monsieur Longereau.

On this occasion I cut out the loudspeaker by the time we got to the second sentence. My mother was pale and a little shaky but reassured somewhere deep down inside her: her feeling of foreboding was right. She no longer need worry now, or nurture any illusions.

"How long ago?" she whispered when I hung up.

"Five months."

She swallowed hard and nodded her head.

"Quite a while, then . . ." she said in a strange fluty little voice with an airy, almost casual note, and she dissolved into tears in my arms, asking why life was always so unfair to her.

I WENT TO SEE HIM ON SUNDAY. In the morning. Row 18, section 3 in the cemetery at Asnière, right next to where they bury the dogs. "Longereau-Beauvoisin Family"—I didn't know who the Beauvoisins were but they shared the marble tomb fifty-fifty. The face that I had glimpsed occasionally while I hid was here in close-up at last in a photo sealed into the stone. And I kept seeing the same image of him over and over again: a silhouette closing a green gate before disappearing into his house. At last I had the right to talk to him. I opened a bottle of champagne, took two glasses from my bag and we drank to each other. I told him all about my life, my own and the one that went with the wig at the bottom of the bag. He couldn't believe his ears. I didn't give him a chance to get a word in. It did me good, I know that. When I said good-bye I left him the bottle and the glasses. He does have a family.

I looked along the rows at the names and dates carved into stone, resuming whole lives. I wondered which stage in my own life I had reached. I always thought I had time to do things, I never thought about death but there and then, that week, I felt surrounded. As I gazed at the picture of a blond woman about my age with fresh roses around it, I pictured my husband leaving a bouquet for me—and to think he never gave me flowers. I ran all the way to a phone booth. A breathless voice answered:

"Yes?"

"I'm sorry to disturb you."

"Who is this?"

"You don't know my name. Never the first time . . ."

I could hear him panting. I thought he was busy making love to someone but, actually, it wasn't that: it was his regular Sunday jog in the Bois de Boulogne. He could cut it short and meet up with me, but just for an hour; afterward he was appearing live on a weekly politics show on TV. I told him that wasn't long enough and it would be better to put it off till another day.

"An hour and a quarter," he bartered.

"One hundred and eighty minutes or nothing at all," I replied uncompromisingly.

He laughed and told me my domineering voice turned him on. We would, therefore, meet up on Thursday, at three o'clock in the afternoon for a window of one hundred and eighty minutes. He gave me the address. I said okay in an authoritative voice and I was the one who hung up.

I didn't know what had come over me. It was a big leap of faith to tell myself this, but I think it was for Roger: for him to think I was still different, hiding things from him, for him to have to work at trying to understand me . . . What was the point fantasizing about a stranger at the movies: he had a far more mysterious woman at home, in his own bed. I realized now how moved I was that he had suspected me of having an affair with his brother, he thought me capable of lying to him, of betraying him in his own family . . . that he thought of me as this monster, as two different women, a sadist . . .

When I arrived home he was worried: his parents were expecting us for lunch and he thought I must have had an accident. He still cared about me and I suddenly felt ashamed for the physical longings I had felt in the cemetery.

"I don't want to go back to my dumb suspicions, Nina, but a church service really doesn't go on for four hours!"

"I was with my father."

"Your father," he said, dropping his car keys. "And exactly how long have you known him?"

"He's dead. We just met."

"What the hell . . . !"

He picked up his keys and turned away from me to check his hair in the mirror. I thought of his bouquet on my grave again, and leaned my head on his back.

"Why don't we say we can't go? We could stay here in peace, we could make love all afternoon . . ."

He turned and took hold of my wrists.

"I just don't know where I am with you anymore, Nina, but I really can't cope with your selfishness any longer. My brother will be there for lunch, I really need to have a reconciliation with him, for him to forgive me, but you . . . all you can think about is fucking."

Gripped with anger, I told him I didn't give a damn about his family: his parents who had cheated on each other and beaten each other up their whole lives before finally getting back together for their old age, or his brother who, yes, it was true, never missed an opportunity to play footsy with me under the table. He went completely red, mouth hanging open, paralyzed.

I immediately regretted my lie, but he suddenly bellowed "I knew it!" and there was such a surge of victory in his voice and so much relief, that I felt I had done the right thing.

He went to his parents all on his own. I spent the afternoon reading magazines, and when he came home he didn't tell me anything about it. He took out a jigsaw puzzle and started building the Great Wall of China.

By a quarter past six he had arranged a dozen stones and put together one cloud. I told him it was very beautiful. His only reply was that his brother was a bastard—rotten through and through like his parents—and he didn't want to see them anymore and, as for us, we would sleep apart. I kissed him on the forehead. I made up his bed on the sofa and told him that if he wanted to come and join me during the night, it wouldn't commit him to anything.

"Imagine I'm a stranger you've spotted, I don't know, in the street, at a café, at the movies, and you could come and make love to me, thinking about her . . ."

For a moment he looked me right in the eye, as if he was teetering on the edge of a chasm. Then he shrugged his shoulders.

"I'm sorry to disappoint you, but there's more to life than just sex." And he went back to his wall.

THIS IS THE THIRD THURSDAY she won't be there. I'm hiding behind the plane tree on the corner by the dry cleaners, watching my husband walking up and down on the sidewalk, crossing the street to make it look as if he has a reason to be there, retracing his steps and keeping an eye on the entrance to the movie theater. A quarter of an hour after the movie starts he goes and asks the guy behind the counter a question; the guy replies with a nod of his head, anything to fill another seat. So he buys a ticket and goes in. I would never have gone to my political meeting if he hadn't gone in, but I feel better for him: given the glimmer of hope that flitted over his eyes, and despite my allusions the other evening, he suspects absolutely nothing and still believes in her.

⟳

I have arrived early, so has he. It's raining. Like last time. He is dressed all in blue and I'm dressed as the *other*—but without the wig. I didn't dare come as myself . . . because of my husband. Or maybe I wanted him to be cheated on by the woman of his dreams. I half wanted that. That's typical of me.

In that red and gold room he hugged me so tightly that the black plastic raincoat squeaked, holding me to him so that he could kiss me. I turned my face away. He looked at me, taut with strain.

"My lipstick will mark your tie," I told him, chilled to the bone by the thought of my husband's tie.

He threw his coat, his jacket, his shirt, and his tie to the floor. I turned out the light. He pressed himself up against me and took my whole mouth into his. I closed my eyes, like in the movies, and I became the *other*. Fully clothed, I slipped down to his knees, against the cold wool cloth of his distended trousers. I opened my lips slightly and waited. In the half light he lowered his zipper. Then I looked right at him, telling myself it was my husband and that he would like this with me. And I swallowed him up.

He stroked my hair but I threw his hands aside harshly. I wanted him to stay passive, completely passive. I went to the very limits of his resistance and, just when he was saying yes, I stopped. I stood back up, threw him backward, straddled him, and ran the rough-edged belt from my raincoat around his neck. I tightened it sharply and watched him orgasm. Then we had a drink together. We had a hundred and sixty minutes left.

⚭

I don't regret what I did. Standing motionless on the tiled floor of the bathroom, dripping in every direction, naked under the plastic raincoat that is now like crocodile skin, I'm looking at myself with satisfaction. In the bedroom, the politician is on the phone explaining that he won't be able to come to parliament: he's pinned to the bed by his lumbago. I wanted *her* to do everything to him. Everything a man would love, dread, and loathe. And she took this man, this powerful man, and turned him into her slave for a day. He's been broken and he's asking for more. He said, "I've never known a woman like you before." She replied, "I know." He added that he was free on Saturday. With the belt of the raincoat around his neck and his diary in his hand, there was something poignant about him. He won't be seeing her again. The only thing that matters to me is that, after what she has just done, my husband won't be able to look her in the eye again.

As I took *her* makeup off, I felt cleansed, purified, intact.

WHEN I WENT TO THE POST office with Gisèle it was their busiest time. The urn was well wrapped and she held it in her arms like a baby. After waiting ten minutes she asked me whether I had a felt-tip pen. I didn't have one but the man behind us in the line very politely offered her his. He was the notary-in-a-duffle-coat type with a double chin and loafers with tassels. She wrote "FRAGILE" in large letters.

"Put 'HANDLE WITH CARE' on the other side, otherwise they won't see it," the man advised her, offering back the pen she had just returned to him. "And also 'THIS WAY UP.'"

"Thank you," Gisèle replied.

But I could see that it was all for my benefit. He was stealing glances at me all the time he was helping Gisèle, like someone stroking a dog to chat up its owner. After what I had done the day before, any man could sense the whore in me, I was sure of it. They just had to look at me and I could see myself spreading my legs on the tiled floor, or sitting astride them, tightening their belts, and then they would see themselves through my eyes.

"Especially if it's glass," he pointed out to me with a knowing nod.

"No, it's porcelain," I said very simply, with no hint of ambiguity.

"Ouch!" he said, grimacing in anticipation the heartache. "It'll break."

Gisèle turned round to give him his pen back, and she said hoarsely but calmly, "No, it won't break. It's emerald green and that's a color that has always brought my mom good luck."

"Oh! it's a present for your mother . . ."

"No, it *is* my mother. And it's a present for my aunt."

"I'm sorry," said the man, wisely immersing himself in the form he had filled in for his certified mail service.

"And, believe me, she doesn't deserve it. But I can't say more about it than that."

"You're next, Gisèle."

She walked up to the counter stiffly, purposefully, like someone stepping up to the altar to communicate. I could feel the notary looking at my buttocks, and I turned right around to catch him at it. He was helping the elderly man behind him fill in a form. I went back to Gisèle with my cheeks blazing. When she saw the little parcel slipping through the window on the counter her teeth started chattering.

"Standard mail or certified?" the girl asked coldly.

Gisèle was still staring at the parcel. She knew this was the last time she would see it. Even though she had kept a couple of ounces of her mother for herself, just over half what was there, stowed in a candy box on the mantle, it was quite something to think the other half was going off to live its life in a postal van. I locked onto her state of mind to try and drive out the images in my head, to erase the pleasure and the shame, to get back to being a normal woman in a real situation. I had to stop thinking I was the focal point here, to forget my furious longing to scream out suddenly in the middle of the post office, "Yes, I came while I half-strangled the congressman for your district, and you can all fuck off!" Too many things that had been held back, buried away, and suffered in silence were clamoring to get out. I didn't want to hide or pretend or lead a double life anymore. I needed scandal, I needed disruption and irreversible changes. But at the same time I still felt the same. I had always been like this: I could never bear to see myself as I really was.

"Standard or certified?" the girl said again, weighing the parcel. "There are people waiting."

I pointed out that it was breakable, and she replied that she wasn't asking whether it was fragile but whether it was urgent.

"Certified," I muttered, clenching my fists.

"No!" Gisèle screamed, her voice increasingly hoarse.

"Gotta know what it is you want!" the girl replied, her mouth distorted with contempt.

Gisèle knocked on the window sobbing, "Give me back my mother! I can't do this to her."

"You're not the only person here, madam! You're wasting my time!"

"This is what you're paid for, bitch!" I launched at her very loudly and perfectly calmly. "You're a public servant, so stop giving me your martyr act behind your little window! Give her back her parcel and smile. Otherwise I'll break the glass down!"

That's how we ended up at the Gare de l'Est railroad station. According to the departures board, the train went to Munich stopping just about everywhere, but most importantly in her aunt's village in Alsace. Gisèle was still stunned by my outburst, trembling as if I'd just saved her life. As for me, I was feeling great. I called my husband to tell him not to wait for me for dinner, and he told me there wasn't any dinner. I explained that I was going with Gisèle to take the urn to her aunt. He told me not to bother inventing excuses. I said okay and hung up. Making his imagination work overtime—it was the only thing I could still do for him. And it made me feel light-headed, liberated. Anyway, I just had to convince myself that all men were masochists, and I was doing them a favor.

It was dark, the coaches were dirty and gloomy, and Gisèle was very quiet. I had yelled so loudly at the post office it had almost taken her voice away. We sat down in an empty compartment with a stuffy smell of old feet. She sat facing me with her parcel on her knees.

"I warn you: I'm going to ring the bell, drop off the parcel, and then we leave," she rasped into my ear.

"Do whatever feels right."

"But you're not to mouth off at her."

"I couldn't give a damn about your aunt, Gisèle."

With a few gesticulations she told me she was going to get something to drink. I offered to look after the parcel for her but she refused, hugging it even closer to her chest. She didn't even recognize me anymore. The only point of reference she had now was her mother, reduced to powder.

The train rumbled through the black night, lurching and screeching, every panel shuddering. It felt like setting off into the unknown, with no hope of coming back. Maybe Alsace was nice. Apart from Ile-de-France in Paris, I only knew Creuse: some walls, a courtyard and a track for country walks. The most interesting boarding school my mother could find, thanks to the rates offered by its council. It was better for my health growing up in the country. She had her life too. And I was the one who had felt guilty, all those years, for complaining about my fate when there were so many poor children in all the pollution of Paris who envied me my fresh air in Creuse. The day I wanted to throw myself off the refectory roof and Gisèle stopped me I swore I would never speak to her again.

I heard a noise in the corridor and got up to go and look, but I couldn't because there was a teenage boy blocking the doorway. He was laughing, holding the parcel open, the cardboard torn apart. Just as I started to drum on the window I saw the little piece of emerald porcelain flying from left to right, thrown by another guy who was grinning as he held Gisèle by her wrists. There wasn't a single sound coming from her, and her long nails weren't of any use to her. She watched the urn flying from hand to hand as they passed it to each other. Then it fell to the floor—broken. Two ounces of Henriette on the grooved rubber.

The train stopped. They kissed Gisèle on the mouth, first one then the other, then they let go of the door where I was still drumming frantically, and they ran off the train. Gisèle was shaking, her eyes staring blankly. I lay her down on the seat but she was afraid to be left alone, so I couldn't go for help. The train set off again and, about half an hour later, the conductor came by. I tried to explain what had happened, but he only spoke German so I gave up. We got off at the first station, in the middle of the night. We went along the underpass to the other platform for Paris-bound trains. There would be a train stopping there in thirty-eight minutes.

Gisèle sat shivering next to me on the bench with her head buried against my shoulder. I would have liked to tell her about my father. . . . Well, about the champagne on the grave, but I just put my arm around her to warm her up in her grief.

✎

"Are you back already?" my husband grunted when I opened the door. He was in his pajamas and had earphones on.

"*We* are," I corrected.

He went back into the living room, and I made some pasta for Gisèle. While the water came to the boil we could hear him talking to himself in Chinese. He wasn't even trying to hide it.

When Gisèle left I went and sat down facing him. His puzzle was coming along well, a few more stones in the Great Wall. I picked up a corner piece and tried to fit it into the sky.

"Leave it alone!"

He took off his earphones to ask what I wanted. I asked him why he was learning Japanese.

"It's Chinese!" he corrected, rather hurt.

"Sorry."

"Was there something you wanted to ask me?"

"Don't you love me anymore?"

"If I didn't love you anymore, I would have left."

The rush of sincerity, honesty, and pain in his voice paralyzed me, I stared at the lid of the puzzle. I heard myself say:

"And I still love you, Roger. Not like before. Maybe better. I don't know . . ."

We sat there in awkward silence, with that weight that had come from both of us. I stared at those few inches of his Great Wall of China. I felt the need to ask him:

"But you have thought about leaving?"

He gave a slow shrug and sighed: "Well, there's the kiosk."

I nodded. We always ask one question too many.

I TOOK THINGS IN HAND again. What we needed was a week's holiday, just the two of us, miles from anywhere and alone in the world. So I set fire to the kiosk—at three o'clock one Monday morning, with a mask, a can of gas, and a box of matches. It wasn't the first time stuff had been burned by vandals in the area. People felt sorry for us but no one was surprised. I called the insurance company to see how much we would get, and I booked a week in Djerba. The best hotel, all-inclusive. That could be our anniversary present.

Roger let me get on with it, his mind was on other things. He couldn't stop grumbling about the bastards who had deprived him of his work. I chose the Thursday morning flight on purpose: a new life was starting for us, one last chance. If we had come to this, if he had wanted to escape reality with fantasies about a stranger, it was because of that stupid job, the numbing routine that had forced us apart by sticking us together. Without the kiosk, there was no longer any need for the Chinese girl. All the same, he did take his earphones with him.

I wanted to present him with another woman in Djerba, to show him everything I had become, because of him and for him. The bridal suite was huge, all mosaics and leather poufs, with a terrace looking out over the sea. He wanted to go for a swim straight away. Then we went down to the restaurant, couscous by candlelight, but he didn't eat a thing because the meal on the flight hadn't agreed with him. I felt gossamer-light in my sequined jellaba. I wanted him the way you want someone you don't know. We couldn't talk because of the music, but I could tell that he was feeling edgy too.

Once back in our room he took his temperature. He had a fever of 103. He spent five days in bed, on antibiotics, with his earphones clamped to his head. I watched him, and told myself it was over. I thought about the wig in the bottom of the bag, in Paris. "She" should have been here instead of me.

We went home two days early, thanks to the cancellation allowed on health grounds. We had hardly spoken a word to each other. On the plane he murmured, "I know you don't love me anymore. Don't bother pretending." I couldn't find anything to say in reply. I think I only started really loving him when he cheated on me with the *other*. But how could I tell him? I had broken enough things in my life.

We rebuilt the kiosk from scratch.

My husband was getting thinner and thinner, but his Chinese was getting better and better. We didn't see his family anymore. He continued going to the movies on Thursdays, but he had stopped hovering on the sidewalk, he went straight in. He had run out of hope, but he had something indestructible left: the knowledge that he had come so close to a kind of happiness that was too big for him, which now took up every inch of him. The *other* had disappeared but I was the one who no longer existed. Monsieur Jean, who had started buying *Le Monde* from me again, could make sure our hands touched all he liked. It no longer had any effect.

I SNEAK INTO THE MOVIE theater and, without making a sound, slip into the seat behind him. He sits up with a start. I nibble the nape of his neck, from right to left, from left to right, and I whisper breathily:

"I've missed you so much."

In the darkness his lips brush past mine. I climb over the back of the seat and kiss him full on the mouth. I close my eyes thinking of the eyeliner traced thickly, oriental style, over my eyelids, of my mouth which is too red, of my soft, soft face powder, of my orchid scent . . . and, between two rows of seats, I let this stranger take me, forgetting that he is in fact my husband.

A deep gasp rises up through me. I wake up with a start.

I am on the sofa. All alone. I jump to my feet. And the *other* is still there making love by the light of the film, crying out in ecstasy in front of everyone with a man whose name she doesn't even know, moaning on the floor among the popcorn and candy wrappers, taut as a bow, her neck arched back, available, so eagerly available . . .

But I'm nothing. I can't bear being just me anymore. I can't bear being both of us anymore. I can't bear her smell of orchids anymore. I open the window and get ready to throw myself out, but I don't want her to win.

⟨∞⟩

When he came home I told him I was the girl in the row behind. He didn't say anything to that so I gave him all the details, and I put on the Chinese accent, I imitated myself to get him to recognize me, finally. But I felt awkward, lumpy, fumbling my words; I could tell I was making a mess of playing myself.

He looked at me as if I was a stranger, then he said coldly:

"And how long have you been brewing this up in your head?"

"First kiss: March 31st."

A look of horror distorted his face.

"Were you there? Did you follow me, right from the beginning, did you . . . ?"

A murderous expression swept over his eyes. And then nothing. His eyes were back to normal, the ones that don't see me. He turned his back on me and walked out of the bedroom.

"I hope you got a good eyeful when you were spying on us," he threw at me over his shoulder.

I held him back.

"It's me, Roger. You fell in love with your own wife, that's all."

"Stop fucking about! Something finally happens in my life, something real, something special, and you think you can mess it up with your stupid fabrications? Do you really think you just have to imitate an accent to make it work? You could never be one tenth of a woman like her, my poor Nina . . . If you knew what she's like when she makes love . . ."

"But you've never made love with her! You can't have! You're lying!"

"You can believe whatever you like."

I heard the front door closing in the hush of the hall. So I went and sat on the same chair as Gisèle's mother, but nothing happened to me. You can't always take someone else's place.

⌇

I didn't sleep all night. I went back over the way we met, the crosswords, the semifinal of "Fun with Prime Numbers" and the sweet simple way we had made love for the first time, and the stupid way I had ended up pregnant straight away. I had invited him to dinner by candlelight to break the news, shaking like I had at school when it was time for confession. He said, "You're not pregnant, are you?"

"Would you mind?"

"Well, yes, I would! You can't start a meal with dessert!"

It was a heartfelt cry. Out of decency, because I didn't want him to feel any obligation, I let the baby go. Neither he nor my mother knew. It hurt but it was my secret.

Now I understood this deep-seated need for a clandestine situation to be able to let go without any shame or fear of predictable reactions: other people's attitudes or disapproval, their pity, their indulgence, the conviction of those who say "If I were you . . ."

When it came down to it, my husband and I both needed the same things, just not together.

He came back to get his things. He had moved into a hotel. I didn't have the address or the phone number. We met when we changed shifts at the kiosk, just like before: the timetable was the same and our customers didn't notice any difference. He was a bit more fired up, that was all. And I was more mousy.

One evening I made up my mind. I went to wait for him outside the movie theater, dressed up as the *other*. He spotted me straight away, from a long way off. We looked at each other for a long time and my glossy, crimson mouth opened slightly in a half smile. Then I stroked my waist and turned my back on him, heading very slowly through the dark streets of Paris toward the Seine. I could feel him behind me, following a few yards behind.

I reached the bridge by Notre-Dame. In a few minutes, when I got to the other side, I would turned around slowly on the square in front of the cathedral, and take off my wig in the glare of the big white floodlights. Then whatever happened would happen. Is there life after the *other*'s death? I wondered.

Halfway across the bridge I heard my name being called.

I stopped, devastated. He had believed me. Or maybe he had never been fooled.

I turned around with tears in my eyes. But it was an old man who was saying "Nina, come here! Heel, heel!"

The little dog scampered back and jumped into his arms.

Roger was on the other sidewalk, he cupped his hands over his mouth and shouted something to me in Chinese. He would never accept the truth.

So I ran across the road, impulsively, blindly. I was running too, like the little dog, with all my strength, faster and faster, hurtling down the steps to the banks of the river, and I threw myself into the Seine saying, "Daddy, it's me." For the first time in my life.

When I came to in the hospital, he was beside me.

"My love," I murmured, "you saved me . . . you jumped in."

He left a moment's silence then, in a neutral voice, he said:

"No, it was a guy in a barge. I was watching the wig floating away, carried by the water. You're alive. But she's dead."

I smiled, feeling equally hurt and happy. The *other* had had a reason to live: by leaving she had given me back my husband, my transformed husband, and she had helped me to become the woman he needed. Everything would change between us now. A new start.

"Roger . . . that woman, she's still me."

He looked at me with clenched teeth and tears in his eyes, then he lowered his head.

"And I'll never forgive you for that."

And he left.